THROUGH A MIRROR DARKLY

Happily. Ever. After.

Through a Mirror Darkly

Roxie Cohen

ISBN: 979-8218240943; 9798218273019

1st Edition

Published by Lavender Fox Press, LLC

915 Summit Street

Bethlehem, PA 18015

www.roxiecohenbooks.com

Playlist

Don't Blame Me–Taylor Swift
You Put a Spell on Me–Austin Giorgio
Falling–Harry Styles
I'll Never Love Again–Lady Gaga
Better Man (Taylor's Version)–Taylor Swift
Love I'm Given–Ellie Goulding
Animals–Maroon 5
Bigger Than the Whole Sky–Taylor Swift
Prisoner (feat. Dua Lipa)–Miley Cyrus
Dark Paradise–Lana Del Ray
Look What You Made Me Do–Taylor Swift
Boyfriend–Dove Cameron
Heartbreak Anniversary - Giveon
I Will Possess Your Heart–Death Cab for Cutie
Gimme What I Want–Miley Cyrus
Dancing With Our Hands Tied–Taylor Swift
No Right to Love You–Rhys Lewis
As It Was–Harry Styles

To Shane—for everything.

TRIGGER WARNINGS

Through a Mirror Darkly is a work of fiction that contains situations and experiences that may be difficult for some readers. Mentions of prior sexual assault are commonly discussed throughout this book. Other triggers include pregnancy loss, stalking, physical assault, and unwanted physical touch. Please reach out to a safe person if the content in this book causes distress. There are resources listed at the end of the book that are available, free of charge, 24/7.

For now we see in a mirror dimly, but then face to face. Now I know in part; then I shall know fully, even as I have been fully known.
- 1 Corinthians 13:12

AUTHOR'S NOTE

Growing up in Appalachia, on the outskirts of The Great Smoky Mountains, has been the greatest privilege of my life. My childhood was barefoot summers, sweet tea, lake days, long drives in the Cherokee National Forest, and picnics in Cades Cove. I've always had an affinity for nature and spent my days running through the trees or lying in the soft grass with my Blue Heeler, Misty.

As a child, we discussed our ancestry frequently. My mom's side of the family claimed to be Cherokee descendants, though I never knew much about it. I did know my mother's stepfather was half-Cherokee, but blood-wise, I didn't know much about my own connection. It wasn't until recently that I learned my grandmother grew up with the Cherokee language spoken at home and the towns I grew up in were once thriving Cherokee communities. I, myself, have no claim to the Cherokee. It's been too many generations at this point. Any blood connection is far too diluted. This missed connection is a loss I will feel forever.

On my father's side, I have the (verified) claim that our ancestor, James White, founded Knoxville, Tennessee. I think of him when I drive down James White Parkway during my visits home. My father's people were known healers and moonshiners in the community. My grandmother's grandfather (Jake) grew poppy plants in his yard that he kept under lock and key. My grandmother said this is a vivid childhood memory. More than once there had been attempts to steal them, making it necessary. My all-time favorite photo of his daughter (my Granny Artie) is of her standing in front of their moonshine still, a wad of cash in her little dirty hands. I'm often left confused and baffled that such a strong Christian man was in and out of jail as a moonshiner, but this was not unheard of in those days in our community. Times have certainly changed.

I grew up in a small town where you couldn't see your neighbor's house from the front porch, let alone play with their kids. My only real friends were the ones I saw at church, my cousins, and my siblings. My dad continues to make the best salsa, and my grandma can sew anything. My mother inherited the grit and tenacity of her mother's people. No matter what life handed her, she survived it. These people, this life, continue to shape me even now.

When Cleo's story came to me, I knew right away it was meant to be set in my mountains. The only question was, how could I choose one specific town? In the end, I couldn't. Instead, I pulled pieces of all of them together to form one place: Shaconage (Sha-Kon-O-Hey). Shaconage was a name deliberately chosen to honor the mountains and the natives who lived there first, who named it first. Shaconage is the Cherokee word for The Great Smoky Mountains, which translates to Land of Blue Smoke.

I encourage you to visit those mountains and experience the beauty of a smoky mountain morning. You won't regret it. If you want to see more of the towns that inspired Cleo's story, visit Townsend, Vonore, Tellico Plains, or Maryville, Tennessee. These are the places that made me and Cleo who we are.

Thank you for reading.

I

Shaconage (Sha-Kon-O-Hey): January

The whistle of the tea kettle echoes through the small, dark, and damp basement. The cellar sinks into the earth as if being swallowed. A single bulb lights the space, casting light into darkened corners. A lumpy futon juts against the sagging steps. Directly against the opposite wall, a television sits precariously balanced on a half-rotted crate. Jars of vegetables and jams line rows of shelving; thick layers of dust cling to the rims. A roll-top desk is shoved beneath the stairs, overflowing with photos and coffee-stained news articles. On the desk, a camping stove holds a battered tea kettle.

The muted voice of a reporter can be heard on repeat as a lone figure continuously replays a news clip. As if hypnotized, the viewer sits, absorbing every detail with absolute stillness.

"On what should have been the most special day of a young couple's life, tragedy struck instead. Cleo Boucher and Vincent DeMarco were married just this afternoon at St. Bart's Episcopal Church."

A reporter stands in front of an old stone church. Dark spires rise toward the sky like a child's hand reaching for forbidden candy. A large archway beckons the visitor to step inside and partake of its sickly sweet desserts. January wind moans as it steps in and out of the coves and crevices of the stone, whipping against the face of the reporter, leaving red welts in its wake.

"En route to the reception, an accident claimed the life of Mr. DeMarco. We have just received word that his wife, Cleo Boucher, is considered critical. The driver, Mark Jeffers, is expected to live. Local authorities have declined to comment further at this time."

The screen flips from the field reporter to a photo on display back at the studio.

"Local photographer, Devin Mathews, was a guest at the wedding and one of the first at the scene of the accident. The photo we are about to show may be sensitive to some viewers."

Ignoring the continued wail of the kettle, the viewer pauses the newscast on a still of the photo, leaning forward to peer closely at the scene.

It is a picturesque display with large oak and magnolia trees bowing under the weight of snow. Untouched banks of pillowed white give the impression of a winter fairy tale. Shimmering like diamonds, icicles drip from branches. Idyllic for a January wedding, if not for the photo's focal point.

At first glance, the two figures at the center of the one-lane highway appear to be embracing. The bride sits with the groom draped across her lap, cradled among layers of tulle and organza.

A closer look, however, gives way to the pain and ugliness of the scene.

Instead of a smile, the bride wears tears. Her once perfectly styled coiffure is mussed; long locks of sunshine fall in blood-matted waves down her back. The gown, once white, is swathed in rivulets of crimson that pool in the center of her abdomen. Her bloody hands grip the man tightly, causing his suit jacket to pucker. Eyes open, but unseeing, the groom's head lolls at an unnatural angle. His arms lie limply at his sides.

Kneeling in front of the small screen, the viewer caresses the face of the bride over and over as the sound of the kettle screams a warning into the night.

2

Phoenix: Thirteen years later

The desert is a calming place. The stillness of the landscape is interrupted only when the dust is kicked up by a breeze. I moved here for this. The quiet. The uninterrupted nothingness. Sure, occasionally I miss regular rainstorms, lush trees, and green grass padding my feet as I walk across the lawn. But the trade-off is worth it. Here, there are no expectations about the woman I'm supposed to be. I can simply exist without strings.

The morning is clear, and I can see fully across the valley toward the mountains from my back garden. I stand in the small patch of grass in the courtyard and stretch while finding my center. I pay twice a year to have weather-appropriate grass sown into the desert soil. The cost is outrageous, but I pay it gladly. I start every morning here, remembering home.

Crossing to my easel and paints, I settle in for a morning of contemplating the landscape. I'm fully aware that I've painted this same scene every morning for a year, and yet, something new grabs my attention every day. Sometimes, it's a simple change in the light; others, a new perspective on an old friend. Or maybe it's simply the yearning for the mountains of my childhood that pulls me in. These ridges couldn't be any more unlike the Appalachian Mountains, yet they are equally mesmerizing in their gruffness.

Dipping a brush into paint, I make the first satisfying stroke across the canvas. Unlike life, paint is forgiving. You can smooth over any imperfection with a couple of simple brushstrokes. As I know all too well, one simple decision in life can irrevocably alter your course forever.

The trill of my cell phone disrupts the silence and breaks my concentration. I glance at my watch. 7:15 a.m. That's too early for a social call. I grab the phone, answering without reading the screen, dread filling me. Only one person could be calling me this early—and for reasons that can't be good.

"What's wrong?" The question is my only greeting. Netta and I are the same. We get to the point.

"Cleo. There's been an accident. It's Dahlia...you need to come home. It's not looking good." Her voice quivers at the end, reminding me that Netta has only Dahlia left in this world.

"What kind of accident?" The last comes out in a slight squeak, my ability to breathe suddenly compromised. "Was it a fall?" I ask automatically, although that doesn't sit well with me. Dahlia is strong. She may be my great-grandmother, but at ninety-three, she has never shown even an ounce of weakness in any way. I can't fathom an existence where Dahlia is anything less than steel.

"No, it's—" she says, hesitating slightly before continuing, "We're not sure. We should know more once you're here. You *will* come?"

The edge in her voice is unsurprising. I deserve it. It's only been thirteen years since I left in the middle of the night.

3

Shaconage: The next day

An hour and a half after leaving the airport, I see the first signs of home. I roll down the window and breathe in the smell of the trees and the river that flows through town, deep into the forest. My rental, a Jeep Wrangler, hums contently as we draw closer to the little mountain town.

I called Netta after landing at five this morning, and we settled on meeting at the home place. There's been no change with Dahlia, and as Netta pointed out, the chickens need tending to. I shake my head, picturing Netta out before dawn, feeding them and lecturing them on politeness and sharing. Like Dahlia, she preferred to homestead her food as much as possible. Since Dahlia is unable to care for them, Netta has taken it upon herself to ensure her friend's darlings are cared for.

The Jeep flows around bend after bend, the shade of the mountain sending chills across the skin underneath my sweat-soaked T-shirt. It's barely dawn, but the summer heat has descended in full force. It may be twenty degrees cooler here than in the desert, but the humidity wins every time.

I pull up to the small 1860s farmhouse I called home until I was eighteen years old and feel my chest constrict. So many memories. Some of them, admittedly, I'd like to forget. I let the Jeep idle for a couple of minutes as I take it all in.

The smell of honeysuckle hits my nose, and I take it in deeply, savoring the sweetness of home. I can't count the number of childhood days spent under the trees, sucking on the flower, chatting away with my best friend, Macy, about the Backstreet Boys and weekend plans at the skating rink. I turn the ignition off and step out of the car, the gravel beneath my feet the only sound I hear.

Quietly, I walk up the path toward the front steps. Dahlia's medicinal herbs keep watch along the borders of the house, reminding me of the past I left behind. *Go away*, they seem to shout. *You don't belong.* I know. *I know,* I tell them. Maybe I never did.

I pause at the foot of the stairs, my heart hammering in my chest. Each boom of my heart sends panic spiraling higher and higher up my throat. My gaze darts around the yard, searching for anything to prolong the inevitable. I'm not ready.

The creak of the screen door, painted a shocking neon green, pulls my focus back to the house, to Netta. Her hair is grayer than when I last her, but she wears the same classic skirt and blouse that I've come to think of as her uniform—cotton and silk. Around her waist sits an apron with deep pockets I know carry the remnants of the chicken seed she recently dispersed out back. Somehow, the contrast between the chicken apron and silk blouse manages to look good on her.

Unable to avoid it any longer, I meet her gaze, apprehension simmering in my gut. I expected anger, maybe even disgust, but I should have known better. Netta doesn't hold grudges, at least not for long. When her eyes meet mine, they mist, and she opens her arms wide. With a sigh, I walk into them. I'm home.

We don't linger at the house. There will be time to revisit memories later. After dropping my bag just inside the door and locking up, we leave for the nearest hospital, situated forty-five minutes away. On the drive, we stay silent. If I'm honest, I'm almost afraid to talk. Netta is grim, and that worries me the most. It's not like her. Netta should be pure sunshine...not this dreary, dark-day version of herself sitting beside me.

Before I know it, we're there. I pull into the visitors' parking and turn off the engine. The building looms large in front of us, and I can't make myself open the door. I cave, turning to Netta. "Tell me what happened," I say firmly, though inside, I'm shaking. What if I don't like what I learn? My gut tenses, then releases as though I'm rolling on a ship, back and forth, fearing I'll capsize at any moment.

She sighs and turns to look out the window. "That's

the thing, Cleo. We don't know what happened. She was found by the mailman, lying face down in the front yard." She pauses, clutching her pearls until her fingers are as white as the strand she wears, before releasing them. I watch as the pink floods back into the tips.

"She was hit with something—in the head—and hurt in other places. I'm not sure of everything." The words tumble out of her, falling over one another to be released. My mind reels with each one, uncomprehending. "I'm sorry, but I didn't want to know it all. It was too horrible. Seeing her like that..." She has tears in her eyes, and I can hear them in her throat, lodged there like cement.

My own voice is a whisper when I finally find it. "You mean—" I start, then stop. Taking a breath that feels entirely too unsteady, I start again. "What are you trying to say?" The idea is ludicrous. There's no one more beloved in Shaconage than Dahlia Boucher. I don't believe it. More than that, I *can't*. Even if the town hated me, and believe me they did, no one hated Dahlia. Dahlia's grandfather settled this very land. Eventually, he named the town Shaconage and built his house, the courthouse, and a church. I don't think there's a single person in Shaconage who hasn't visited our house as a part of a school-mandated historical tour. Dahlia Boucher was practically royalty here. It was unbelievable.

Netta gives me a sad look, her big eyes swallowing her face. Was she always this pale? She takes a breath, and when she starts to speak, I lose mine.

"Honey, someone has been harassing her for months.

She didn't tell anyone but me." She laughs, the sound brittle and harsh. "Only in the last week did she even do that." She shakes her head and takes my hand in hers. "Threatening notes have been left at the house. You know how she is. She brushed it off." At this, she shrugs and waves her hand in dismissal.

I get it. Of course, Dahlia would brush it off. That's just who she is. I turn to look up at the dark building, muted light beckoning me inside.

"At least, until the notes started talking about you."

I almost break my neck, I swivel so fast to look at her and feel my eyes as they open impossibly wide, the skin tightening around the edges. I feel strangled, my breath slipping from my body as I sit there, unable to process this new information.

"Notes about me?" The words sound hollow, and I fight hard as my mind tries to dissociate. *Get it together, Cleo. Dahlia needs you to be present.* "Who's sending them?"

Netta shakes her head and sighs. "We don't know who's been sending them. I've been over this so many times with the sheriff. He's handling it, Cleo."

I nod. Gordon is a good man. If Netta says he's handling it, then it's handled.

It's half past eight when we finally exit the Jeep and go inside. The hospital is quiet at this time of day. A small relief. Once we've checked in at the desk, I race ahead to the intensive care unit, leaving Netta to make her own way. I pretend I don't notice the stares as I pass. There are plenty of reasons I left Shaconage and even fewer of them to spend lingering on old memories. I've moved on with my life. More than that, Dahlia is the most important thing at present. She's all that matters to me here.

For all my rushing, I pause at the doorway. I count to ten. My eyes bore into the light-colored wood, but my hand remains motionless on the knob. I've been here before, standing at a door in this unit. Each time, death awaited on the other side. My parents, my little sister Cecily, grandparents, and even Vincent. All gone, some of them for so many years, I can't recall their faces.

A quick look at my hand confirms it's shaking. I take deep breaths, willing it to calm. My mind starts to wander as I breathe, drifting away to another place where memories of a day long ago intrude.

I'm five years old, and I'm in kindergarten. Sitting in the nurse's office, I'm seated on a cot. My hand has a freshly applied Band-Aid, and my hands are sticky from holding the biggest lollipop I've ever seen. I've been humming, content to wait until the nurse could walk me back to class.

There's a knock on the door, and the nurse steps away to answer it. I watch her frown and put her hand to her mouth. She darts a glance at me, and I peer around her to see the principal with tears in her eyes. They look at me.

"Cleo," the principal calls to me. "Come with me. You have a visitor in the office."

I hop down and start toward the door, focusing on the squeaking noises my shoes make on the floor. The school nurse, Miss Nina, stops me and hugs me tightly. I hug her back, a huge grin forming on my face. She's nice.

Following Miss Mills, I skip to the office and, for once, she doesn't scold me to walk carefully. Just inside the door, I see Dahlia and rush ahead, flinging myself into her arms with a giggle. Dahlia is my absolute favorite person. She rubs the top of my head, and I laugh as I look up at her, happy to see her here. Only when I see her face, she's not laughing too.

She leans down to look me in the eyes, her soft hand cupping my face. "Cleo, you're going to come live with me now." She doesn't say anything more, and I don't know how I know, but suddenly, I feel their absence. Mom. Dad. Nanny. Pap. Cecily. They were all gone.

"Cleo?" Netta has caught up, her voice forcing me back to reality. I sway a bit on my feet as I reorient myself. I don't bother to reply. I push open the door and step in.

The small woman in the bed is unrecognizable. Was she always this small? Her head is wrapped in white bandages that taper off around her forehead. There's a large cut on her face that's been stitched, her right eye, black. A cast encases her left arm and leg. She is not awake. "Has she been conscious at all?"

Netta steps forward and takes my hand. "No, she hasn't opened her eyes even one time. They aren't sure she will." Her words strangle any response out of me. She could *die.* Who would do this? The cuts and bruises on her body, the black eye and broken bones have me rushing down the hall to the visitors' bathroom. I make it into a stall just in time to lose what was left of breakfast. Turning my back to it, I simply lie on the tile, feeling it press into my cheek, icy pinpricks piercing my tear-stained cheeks.

After a while, I pull myself up on shaky legs to rinse my mouth in the sink. The taste of vomit lingers, but I can't find it in me to care enough to rinse again. I stare into the mirror for what feels like years, though I know it's only minutes. With a deep breath, I smooth my hair back into its ponytail and wipe my face with a wet paper towel. I practice a smile in the mirror, as I often do. *Fake it until you make it, Cleo.*

When I return to Dahlia's room, Netta has stepped out. I tiptoe over to the bed and crawl into it with her, resting my head on her shoulder. Between sobs, I whisper all the things I wish I had said years ago.

Netta stays with her when I head back to the house to find the letters. When Dahlia told her about the threats, she didn't share the letters. They must be somewhere in the house. Netta wasn't happy that I want to investigate the attack myself, despite my efforts to explain the need to do something, *anything* to help.

"Cleo, Dahlia would not want you putting yourself in danger like this. She'd be furious. She'd tell you to pack up

and go back to Arizona. I shouldn't have brought you here. She'll never forgive me if something happens to you, too."

I'm Dahlia's only living family. Netta isn't technically related to us, but she's been Dahlia's best friend since they were girls. Like Dahlia, she has only me. Netta lost her husband early in marriage and never considered another man. She's a lot like me in that regard. We linger. I shake off thoughts of Dahlia and Netta and turn my attention to the steep mountain peaks in front of me.

Those looming towers remind me of a fortress, hiding people and their secrets deep inside. The desert has changed me more than I thought. There was a time that these mountains provided nothing but safety. Now their familiarity feels like prison walls the farther I navigate within the trees. Eyes darting to the rearview mirror, I watch as the highway disappears around the curving road, the hills curling me tight within.

Instead of taking a right toward home, I jerk the wheel to the left at the last minute, taking a winding route farther up the mountain. My stomach squeezes into knots, and I try not to think of what I'm doing. Instead, I puff out quick bursts of air and try to control my breathing the way they teach in meditation class. *Focus on breathing, Cleo. You can do this.*

The drive is short, yet each moment drags as my mind screams to turn around. *You're not ready for this, Cleo. You never will be.* Around a deep bend, I swerve to the right and slam on the breaks, my body jerking at the sudden assault. With shaky hands, I rub a hand over my chest and massage the area where the belt tightened. That will bruise.

The road is narrow, but the Jeep is only parked partially in the road when I step out of it. Immediately, my eyes land on a white object. The grass around the cross is cut down, while the untamed grass grows tall and gnarled all around the ditch around it and into the bank and trees lining the road. Taking a seat on the grass in front of the small cross, I run my fingers over it. The name "Vincent DeMarco" is delicately carved into the wood. Most likely done by someone in town to honor a favorite son.

There are no tears. The truth is, I barely knew him. Vincent was kind and honorable, that much is fact. He saved me, even if I couldn't save him in the end. Absently, I twist the silver band on my left hand. Sitting here makes it impossible to avoid memories of our wedding day. It was a beautiful service. Vincent's parents made sure of that. While I may have been undesirable as a daughter-in-law, they had no intention of admitting it to the entire town.

The heaviness of the ball gown sits on my shoulders, even now. Most brides feel happy on their wedding day, but that was not my experience. I felt only fear. Not fear of Vincent, but of being trapped. And that's what I was, a scared little trapped rat.

I can feel it now—the veil covering my face, hiding the dark circles and tight lips. Mrs. DeMarco whispering in my ear. The small pinch she gave me as she told me to smile. The disapproval in Vincent's grandmother's stare and the side glances between the women as I walked down the aisle, gloved hands covering their mouths as they gossiped about me. About *my* future. About my *life*.

"Look at that Cleo Boucher, she thinks she's something."

"How did she trap one of the DeMarco boys?"

"I didn't even know she knew who Vincent was."

"She certainly gets around."

"Wasn't she always running after the other boy? She must really want that DeMarco money."

And then it was over—no grand gestures, no butterflies, and no feeling of contentment or happiness. A small kiss and it was simply done.

The sound of tires on asphalt snaps me back to the present. Standing, I brush the grass from my knees before turning to see the familiar sight of the sheriff's truck. A smile of greeting dies on my lips when the occupant steps out.

Ben DeMarco. *Shit.*

4

There was a time when the sight of Ben DeMarco sent goosebumps down every inch of my skin. A time when the sound of his voice could melt my insides like a volcano erupting into rivers of lava, leaving me feverish and desperate. Someone should tell my traitorous heart that those days are long gone because it's pounding out of my chest right now, just like the old days.

The sound of the river pulses between us as he takes his time walking across to me. Feeling unsure of his reaction to my presence here, I glance nervously at Vincent's memorial before lifting my gaze to his face. It's impossible to read his expression hidden behind the sunglasses, but his tensed jaw says everything I already know. He despises *me*. Unbelievable.

"Of course, you'd be here. I knew it was only a matter of time before your guilt ate you up, and you came crawling back." His tone is venomous. Any response dies in my throat as I stare at his fist. The long fingers and calloused palms I once knew so well are curled impossibly tight. A part of me, a secret part I can't acknowledge, aches to unfurl his fingers and soothe away the hurt. Of course, that would never work, not when I'm the reason he's in pain.

I find my voice, clearing the knot that's suddenly closing my throat. "Ben. I didn't know you were back in town—and sheriff, too. Interesting." What an understatement. Ben hated everything about this town, its society, and his family's standing here. Interesting doesn't begin to cover it.

"What I find interesting, Cleo, is that you think Dahlia or Netta or anyone in this town needs you here at all. Even more of a puzzle is you sitting here, next to a memorial for my dead brother like you give a damn about him or anyone other than yourself." The words make me flinch, but I don't speak. He's not looking for a response from me anyway. "Did you seriously think we'd want you back, that we've thought of you even once since you bailed on everyone and everything you once claimed to love?" He's in my face now, his brilliant blue eyes, darkened to storm clouds, staring into mine. Every word out of his mouth is cold and clipped, and it's impossible for me to stop the shiver that slides down my spine.

He's not wrong. I wasn't able to stay here after Vincent died, in this place that reminded me of my selfishness and pain. I left without telling Dahlia or Netta, before Vincent's funeral even, and I hadn't been back once since then. Thirteen years is a long time to expect forgiveness or even welcoming arms.

The whispers were fierce leading up to our wedding. Considering I was dating Ben until a month before I married his brother, well, who could really fault a little gossip? I knew my reasons for the marriage, and so did Vincent. Ben, on the other hand, never got the full story. His hatred of me, at least on that end, is justified. A promise is a promise, and when I married Vincent, I gave my word that Ben would never know why we married so hastily. Say what you will about me, but I keep my word.

The corners of my mouth tilt into a smile. It's the only defense I have, and if I don't do something, I know I'm going to cry. "Oh, Bennett. As if I could ever need you. I'm here for Dahlia, nothing more. As soon as I get her back on her feet and her assailant caught, I'll leave for good, and that's a promise." Queasy but more confident now, I take a step back and force my spine to stiffen like armor. Cleo The Bitch is a character I can play well.

"I would have preferred to discuss this with Gordon, but it seems I'm stuck with you instead. It's all the same." Dismissive, I wave my hand in his direction to indicate the inconvenience of his presence. "I need to know about those letters, Ben." He stares at me for a long moment, and I have to force myself to keep quiet. *Stay calm, don't make this personal. Wait him out.*

It's clear he wants to tell me to go to hell, but instead of doing that, he gives me a tight nod before crossing briskly to his truck, slamming the door, and peeling out before I even move a step. The smell of rubber hits my nostrils a second before he disappears around the bend. Knees buckling, I sag to the ground, hand pressed to my heart where I feel the wound, fresh as ever, pulsing back at me.

Upon arriving at the station, I find Ben pacing in front of the two desks that occupy the front office—one for the receptionist and the other for his single deputy, who was probably seated at Pop's diner right now, enjoying a hot ham and cheese. It was 12:30, and small-town crime is not really a thing. Well, most of the time. My presence here now is proof that it exists. My chest constricts as I think about Dahlia lying alone in her hospital bed. Pulling open the door, I make my way slowly to him, watching as he continues his route between the desks.

When he catches sight of me, I watch as his body jerks away from me, like a dog unexpectedly meeting a rattlesnake on a hiking trail. It's jump or get bit. *Better the snake than the prey.* He motions for me to sit, and I do, perching stiffly on the edge of the yellow plastic chair. A vague memory of the same yellow chair from the school cafeteria hits me: Ben, lounging in the chair, as he laughs at my popsicle jokes.

Around the room are other cast-offs from our school days. A chalkboard with an uneven green splat in the lower right corner is on the otherwise bare wall by the entrance. Jeff Jones was suspended for a week after throwing that paint at Harper Reeves. The desk in front of me is the same one I sat at with Dahlia when I learned about my parents. I remember staring at the intricate grooves, imagining a river flowing through them, carrying me far away.

He clears his throat, so I force my gaze back to him. His blue eyes are calmer now, assessing me in a way that makes me squirm in the plastic seat. His hair is still a brilliant shade of black, though I notice one or two white hairs around the temple, reminding me of an article I read on stress-induced premature graying hair. Any comment on it dies in my throat when he walks around the desk to stand in front of me. When standing, his height doesn't intimidate me much, since I'm five foot ten, but sitting those four extra inches makes me feel small.

My face burns when I realize he's waiting for me to speak. Not at all comfortable with the scrutiny, I make a sweeping gesture at the room. "Why does your office look like a high school classroom?" Every piece of furniture is at least twenty-five years old, including the yellow chair I currently inhabit.

He shrugs. "Budget cuts. My parents donated a large sum for new desks and supplies down at the school. These were kindly donated."

"I'm guessing your parents didn't extend the same favor to the sheriff's office?"

"Hardly. Dad still has some hope that I'll join the family law firm one day." He doesn't say *like Vincent*, but the words hang there between us anyway. Eyes burning with unshed tears, I look down at my hand where the silver band sits dull on my finger. I touch it gently before sitting back up and rubbing my thighs one, two, three times—a small ritual that I've found calms me.

"So." I look at him expectantly, causing him to sigh. He runs his fingers through his thick hair and down his face before replying.

"I don't think it's a good idea for you to be involved in my investigation, but I have to admit you might be useful." He pauses, his gaze turning to the trees outside the window. "Maybe you can help decipher some of these messages, see something we're missing." He goes quiet as if he's turning the possibilities over in his mind. After a moment, he turns back to me, his mouth unsmiling. "Before we get started, you need to know that your involvement is 'need to know' only, and I won't tolerate your interference in my investigation. Got it?"

"Got it," I say quickly, eager for more details. I will tentatively agree to anything at this point. I can always renegotiate later.

After one final long look at me, he unclips the stack of papers that were neatly assembled in piles around his desk and fans them out. The first set of papers appears to be official documents with Shaconage Sheriff's Dept. stamped in the upper left corner. The second set is witness statements, signed by both the officer taking and the witness providing the statement. I start to take the closest set when my gaze snags on an accordion file Ben pulls from the drawer.

One by one, he withdraws photos and lays them out slowly, pieces of my life that I study with detached curiosity: Dahlia's kitchen, the mailbox, my bedroom, the front door. What finally unravels me is a photo of Dahlia sprawled across the walkway, legs bent, and arms pinned. There is so much blood that I can't stop myself from releasing a small whimper.

Unconsciously, my hand caresses my abdomen in slow circles. The control I've been tightly clinging to begins to crumble. I'm on the verge of losing my shit. He doesn't look at me at all, though I can sense he's aware of my distress. He doesn't comment on it. A slight relief.

"Before we go further, I have a couple of questions." A brief nod is my only reply. "To your knowledge, does anyone hold a grudge against your family?"

"A grudge...against Dahlia?" I laugh. What a ridiculous question.

Without commenting, he continues, "Has anyone made any threats toward you?" My head snaps up at that, my eyes leaving the photos to search his face. His eyes are tight, and it's clear there's something he's not telling me.

"Ben. What's going on?" My words are nothing more than a whisper. He pulls away from me, and I drop my hand. It's not until then that I realize I reached for his hand. I sit back, embarrassed, slipping into a practiced mask of indifference: bored eyes, neutral mouth, slouched posture. *Check.*

It doesn't go unnoticed. He shakes his head as though I'm a disappointment to him and pulls a white envelope from the file. "This photo here shows the last letter Dahlia received." Leaning forward once more, I peer down at the photo. "The envelope was in her pocket, sealed and neatly tucked. As you can see, there's no stamp. We assume it was hand delivered." I scoot my chair closer, all pretense of indifference forgotten, as I pick up the letter. I gasp when I read the name of the addressee.

Cleo Boucher was written in block lettering across the front. My eyes jump from the page to his.

"What does it say?" The agony in my voice is unmistakable. Something tells me I don't want to know the answer, and yet I know I must face it.

Ben reaches into the envelope and pulls out a single sheet of copy paper. My hands shake as I take it.

Dear Cleo,

I'm sorry to bring you home like this. I know this will make you unhappy, but you've left me with no choice. You weren't coming back on your own, and I've waited 13 years for us to be together at last.

There are some lessons you need to learn, Cleo. You hurt me, and for that, you have to suffer. Dahlia's sacrifice is your atonement. For the wages of sin is death, and someone had to die.

I'll see you soon.

I re-read the letter, looking for any clues as to the identity of the sender but find none. I did this. Dahlia's accident—not an accident at all, but a murder attempt—was because of me. The world dips, and I feel as though there is a stone in my gut. Standing abruptly, the movement knocks the yellow chair over. Paying it no mind, I stumble out of the door. Barely two steps outside, I fall to my knees, my hands covering my mouth to make the screams quiet. The tears start, and I don't know how long I'm there before I hear Ben exit.

From the corner of my eye, I see his boots next to me, but I keep my head bowed. I can't bear to look at him. Eventually, he lowers himself to the ground, leaning against the wall next to me.

Silently, he offers a box of tissue and a bottle of water. There's nothing left to say, really, so we say nothing at all. When I can stand, I walk slowly to the Jeep and don't look back.

5

I don't like who I am here, in Shaconage. The things that people love about me in Arizona, in the artist community, are lost here. It's as if the growth I've experienced professionally, and even emotionally, doesn't exist. In this place, I'm a pariah.

I've been lying for hours in the twin-sized bed of my childhood, yet sleep mocks me. I've replayed the events of the day over and over in my head. The stares I received in the hospital weren't entirely unexpected. If even for a brief time, I was a DeMarco, and that means something here. The tragic circumstances of Vincent's death make me even more of a curiosity to them.

What I hadn't anticipated was the effect Ben's reaction would have on me. The look of disgust on his face affected me more than I knew it would or even could. Every time I close my eyes, I see the way his lips pressed into a line any time he looked at me. It's easy to imagine the sound of his teeth grinding together behind his clenched jaw with the effort it took to avoid insulting or yelling at me. No matter how much I will it away, the images linger, shaming me.

What hurt more than the reactions of Ben or those in town was the discovery that Dahlia had cleared out my childhood bedroom. Not a single personal item remains of me in this house. Did she burn my Simple Plan and Britney Spears CDs? Did she toss my childhood quilt? It's entirely possible she donated the blanket to the local Goodwill and that some other little girl is curled up in it right now. Or perhaps, every piece of me lies at the bottom of a landfill, becoming more rotted and unrecognizable with each passing day. Forgotten. Unwanted. Useless.

The only sign that I ever lived here at all are the carved initials CB + BD 4-EVA at the base of the headboard. It was the first thing I checked, dropping to my knees and running my fingers over the letters like a prayer. A strangled laugh left my throat at proof that my memories were real. I had existed here.

Heart heavy, I toss and turn in the bed for a bit longer until it becomes obvious any further attempt at sleep tonight is useless. With a sigh, I throw back the blanket and stumble down the short hallway to the kitchen. The appliances, including a mixer older than me, remain unchanged in the small space. I run my fingers over the rounded edges of the can opener, remembering the canned tamales Dahlia would make me on rainy Saturdays. We'd melt a single slice of American cheese on top. Dahlia called it "The Rainy-Day Special." The corners of my mouth lift at the memory of a forgotten childhood delicacy.

On autopilot, I take a glass from the cabinet and fill it with water from the tap. Taking a big gulp, I cradle the glass as I walk to the front room. A bookshelf takes up most of the room. Its shelves are packed with novels and biographies, even some photography collections. As a child, I would sit by the fireplace with books on classic and modern art, thinking of all the ways I could edit them to make them mine.

The wall opposite the bookshelf, where my high school art once hung, is covered in commercial prints. A search of the room reveals no sign of my work. Other than the floral couches and a couple of end tables, there's nothing else in the room. Disappointment cuts like a knife, sudden and sharp. There seems to be nothing left of me here at all. What if Dahlia doesn't want me here?

Emotion is a tricky thing. Coming back to Shaconage was never a priority for me, and I might not have come back for several more years. Maybe not even until Dahlia died. It's not exactly something I'm proud of, but it's the truth. Despite that, the thought that Dahlia might have abandoned me cuts deep.

It's always been the two of us against the world, crushing and conquering anything and everything that came at us. Though, I suppose, she's been on her own for over a decade, dealing with the fall-out I left behind. She doesn't owe me a damn thing. And yet, she never sounded angry or disgusted when we spoke on the phone. She was supportive, proud even, of the life I built in Arizona.

Why, then, am I a ghost in this house?

I sit in silence on the old, worn couch for the rest of the night, wracking my brain to think of *anyone* who could have been harboring romantic feelings for me, but no one comes to mind. How am I supposed to respond to this insane declaration of love if I don't know who it could be? How can I protect Dahlia from someone that doesn't exist in my memories?

By morning, I'm pacing the floors. To my surprise, Dahlia kept my high school yearbooks, but despite pouring over every photo and note within, nothing alarming stands out. The books lie discarded across the floor, but I barely glance at them as I continue my anxious trek.

Desperate for a distraction, I call to check in on Dahlia, but nothing has changed. She still hasn't opened her eyes, which means we still have no answers. An ache settles like a stone in my gut, reminding me that this isn't a problem I can fix easily—no matter how much I might wish otherwise.

"Ms. Boucher, I don't have any treatment updates to give you, but you can certainly speak to the doctor tomorrow when he visits for rounds. Since this is Sunday, he won't be in. You are welcome come to visit and spend time with Ms. Boucher, but she remains unconscious at this time." The nurse pauses as if debating her next words. She clears her throat and sighs. "Your grandmother's friend is still here. I wasn't sure if you were aware. She's been sleeping on a cot in the room. She rarely leaves the hospital and at her age...well, maybe you can convince her to go home and get some rest tomorrow."

Poor Netta. Disappointment at my carelessness hits me, adding to a never-ending wave of self-loathing. *Great job, Cleo.*

"Thank you so much," I hear myself say. "I'll come by tomorrow and convince Netta to go home for some rest. Maybe she'll be more willing to go home if we get some reassurance from the doctor." I hang up, reminding myself to call Netta early this morning and beg for grace I know I don't deserve.

The first signs of the rising sun peek over the mountaintops, casting light into the trees at the edge of the yard. I feel small tendrils of hope stirring despite the desperate situation we're in. Taking a break to paint for a while might help me reset and find clarity. While I might not know who I am in this now foreign landscape, at least I know my place in this world when it comes to paint.

The sound of my bare feet is muted on the hardwood as I hurry down the hall to my room. In the closet, I find my suitcase; I quickly pull it out and fling it on the bed. Inside, I find one of two flat canvases and my travel art set. Grabbing them, I jam my bare feet into sandals before making my way outside. The walk is mostly silent, but the occasional conversation of birds filters through the quiet to sing in my ears. My trek takes me deeper and deeper into the trees where I used to play.

A sudden memory of running through the trees, pretending to be Pocahontas, greets me. I smile, remembering how I broke my arm after jumping from a branch to the soft dirt. A high break that wasn't even cool enough for a cast, I remember telling Dahlia. Instead, I got a sling covered in teddy bears. Dahlia locked my bike in the shed when she discovered I'd been riding it against the doctor's orders.

The sound of chirping in the trees calms me as I walk toward my destination, and the soft gurgles greet me before I see the brook. My favorite spot has a thick layer of grass covering it now, and I feel some satisfaction knowing it remains unknown to others. I take a seat on the cool grass, remove my Chaco sandals, and dip my toes in the cool water. The shock of the early morning chilled water greets me and sends goose pimples up my calves.

I simply sit and breathe for a while. At some point, I start to paint, though I hardly recall the transition from meditation to painting. Most days, they feel the same. To a stranger, I'm sure the canvas would look formless, childish, as though it's been created by a five-year-old. Soon, though, I know the jumbled swirls and knots will come together to create a beautiful tribute to this brook. If only I can find the patience to trust the process. I continue to add strokes, slowly and meticulously, while my heart settles and finds a gentle rhythm.

Lunchtime comes quickly, and I reluctantly pack things away, sliding my paints into the khaki satchel I've carried for the last twenty years. The zipper is long gone, and the top flap and inner lining have been fraying for at least ten. It's been mended so many times, it hardly resembles the bag Dahlia bought me so long ago. The canvases are awkward and bulky in my arms, and I pause, almost stumbling over my feet, when I realize I've been humming.

A feeling of something close to peace has cocooned me, which I find a welcome surprise. Touched, I take a moment to study my surroundings, drinking in the home that shaped me. These mountains haven't given up on me, so I won't either. A feeling of hope and a sense of urgency wells within me to do whatever it takes to make this home safe for Dahlia again.

The screen door is open when I reach the back of the house. I can hear the sound of a radio in the kitchen and Johnny Cash's familiar croon floats across the backyard to greet me. With a grin, I increase my pace, taking the last two steps in a jump, and open the squeaky door.

I know my grin is likely maniacal, but I can't help it.

"Macy!" Standing at the stove, two steaming mugs in her hand, is my best friend. She gives me a gentle smile. It isn't until I see her that I realize I need a friend. Then I'm crying, and she's holding me, giving comforting small rubs as she makes soft *shh* sounds.

Reluctantly, I pull back and inspect her. She looks the same, but also completely different. Her dark hair, once long and wild, lays in a flattering pixie cut, showcasing her thin face and matching dark eyes. When we were young, she seemed to shrink into herself. The woman in front of me now carries herself tall and confident.

"I'm so sorry about Dahlia. Netta called this morning

and told me you'd come home. I'd have called you but..." She trails off, and I wince. No one from Shaconage but Dahlia and Netta have my current phone number. It's not a secret exactly; it's listed as my contact number on my website, though most inquiries come by email. I rarely deal with calls.

"I'll give it to you now." I grab a sticky note and jot it down, folding it and handing it to her. She smiles at me, a dimple appearing on her left cheek, before tucking it into the pocket of her slacks.

The truth is, I cut out everyone when I left town years ago. It's true that Macy is my best friend, but other than some casual messages on Facebook, we have had little to do with one another since. Not that she hadn't tried, because she did. For months, she'd sent messages I ignored. Sitting here with her now, I regret severing our friendship so quickly.

"Do you remember that old house we loved as kids?" I sag in relief when she changes the subject, grabbing onto the change in topics like a lifeline.

"The one on Pinto Peak?" I remember it well. We used to sneak liquor from her mom's house and drink it up there, listening to music on her CD stereo. We'd camp out all night under the stars, laughing and talking about the future.

Her playful smile breaks into a big grin. "The very one! I bought it-I guess I've had it for about five years now. Most of the interior has been completely remodeled, and I've lined up a guy to start on the siding later this summer."

"Wow, that's amazing! You always said you'd buy it, and you did."

She pulls out a cell phone and pulls up renovation photos. The look is spectacular. She flips by a photo of a nursery quickly, her eyes darting to mine. She blushes and looks away.

"You'll have to see it. It's honestly just a perfect space. Dahlia has seen it and even gave me some design tips."

My smile drops at the mention of Dahlia, and she sees it before I can fix it. She takes my hand. "How is she? No one can stop talking about it. I can't imagine it could be anyone local. Was it a robbery?"

I'm not sure how much I'm allowed to share with others. If it's not already common knowledge, it's probably not a good idea to share details about the threatening notes.

"The sheriff isn't sure what's going on yet, and I don't think he has any suspects, at least not any he's willing to share with me." I hope I sound truthful. The last thing I want is to alienate the only person actually happy to see me.

Ugh. Screw Ben. I need answers.

"Uh, Mace. Have you been in touch with Dahlia lately?" It's difficult, but I manage to keep my voice steady as I ask.

"I see her weekly at church, of course."

I nod. I must be the only person in this town who doesn't attend church anymore. "Right. At church. Has she mentioned any worrying conversations or problems with anyone in town?"

Macy frowns while she twirls her necklace around a finger. "You know, I was here a few weeks back, to check in on Dahlia, and saw an old brown truck leaving. The driver wasn't anyone I recognized, but I thought nothing of it until now. Dahlia wasn't even home, and she mentioned no missing items or concerns when I did see her."

I file this information away, reminding myself to mention the truck to Ben next time I see him.

Macy shifts in her seat, and I watch as her right knee starts to bounce. She begins to speak a couple of times but stops. Finally, she asks, "Are you still painting?"

"Cut the crap, Mace. What do you want to know?"

She lets out a sound, a cross between a laugh and a snort, and shakes her head. "I was just wondering...how did it go with Ben? You referred to him as 'sheriff' and haven't said another word about him."

"How do you think it went? I married his brother, and now he's dead. Not only did I leave town, but I left before Vincent's funeral. When he came home, it was to a broken family. So, no, he wasn't exactly thrilled to see me." I say this with what I imagine is dripping sarcasm.

"You forgot to mention that you two were also an item before you married Vincent. That might have something to do with it, too." She says this accusingly, one finger pointed at me. It's so comical, I'd laugh if the subject weren't so serious.

"He left me. Don't forget it. If he hadn't, I never would have ended up with Vincent, and you know it. He probably does too. So, yes, he has some right to hate me, but I have just as much reason to loathe him." My tone is calm, and my voice is even. Somehow, I've managed to convince even myself that I'm unaffected. It's impossible to count the nights I've lain awake thinking of how different life might have been if Ben had been a better man, and I hadn't been weak. Sure, he left, but I *am* the reason his brother is dead. It's true that I hadn't killed him, but if he hadn't just married me and been in that car, Ben would still have a brother, and I might still have a home.

Macy nods, and the sympathy I see in her eyes blinds me. No one knows I didn't love Vincent, that I never stopped loving Ben. Not even Macy. After my husband died, I couldn't stay in Shaconage—a place that was smothering me before he died and strangling me soon after. Call me a coward, but I couldn't face the hate.

Vincent was the town's golden boy. And deservedly so. He was selfless and kind. He was hardworking, driven, and he loved his family, above all else...which is exactly how we ended up married in the first place.

My stomach knots as thoughts swirl of our wedding day, his beautiful smile and his eyes as I watched life leave them. Nausea wells up, and I desperately want to crawl in a hole somewhere and bury myself. Of course, I don't do any of that. Instead, I smile and change the subject.

"So, tell me about this nursery." I gesture toward her phone, and I watch as a flush creeps across her cheeks, staining them a soft pink.

"Oh! Well, I'm just thinking ahead. I've been seeing someone special for a while now, and we're going to take the next step. We just want to be prepared." Her face is cherry red, and I can't help but giggle. It's infectious, and soon we're both laughing and snuggled close on the couch, while she shows me photo after photo of her new home and talks of her plans.

We talk about little nothings until well into the night.

After Macy leaves, I take a shower and clean up the dinner dishes. As I lock the front door before bed, a flash in the trees has me stopping in my tracks. I see the light twice more, in quick succession. I linger a few minutes longer, heart pounding in my chest, but it doesn't happen again. With a flick, I turn the porch light back on. Then I bolt both the front and back doors before finding my bed. It's not until hours later that I startle awake.

Someone was taking photos of the house.

6

After visiting Dahlia this morning, I'm at loose ends. There's been no change since her accident, and I'm rapidly losing hope. I try to think positively, but in the back of my mind, I can't help but ask myself what I'll do if she never wakes up. Desperate to escape these thoughts, I drive aimlessly through town.

A stop at the sheriff's office proves unfruitful when I'm informed by the deputy on duty that Ben is not in. Surprisingly, the deputy is the same one that drove us home when we were sixteen and caught drinking down at the river. Is it weird for him to be forced to work for a kid he once arrested? I leave a message along with my phone number.

As I drive through the small downtown, memories hit me in quick succession. Some memories revolve around Dahlia, others Ben or Macy. Sprinkled among them are the faded, cherished memories of my parents, Cecily, Nan, and Pop.

Pop used to take us to the park on Sundays. Most families were in church, but not Pop. He never had much use for organized religion. Instead, on Sundays we would have a picnic there, and he'd take turns swinging us on the swing set. Cecily was younger than me, but she liked to go the highest. I was always afraid to soar too high, worried I'd fall.

I had my first kiss at the theater downtown. It was a one-room establishment that was mostly inhabited by local teens on Friday and Saturday nights. There wasn't much to do in Shaconage, and we were lucky to have even one movie playing weekly. That first kiss was with Ben, of course, when I was seventeen. We'd gone to a slasher flick, and I remember scooting closer and closer to him as the killer closed in on the hero. Ben wrapped me in his arms, squeezing me tight.

For the rest of the show, he held me there, rubbing small circles on my wrist with his fingers. After the movie ended, and we were the only ones left in the room, he kissed me for the first time. My lips tingle at the memory of that first press of lips against mine and the feeling of his breath on my cheek.

At the end of Main Street sits the grocery store, where I'm headed now. You know it's a small town when the grocery store is a hardware-gas station-grocery store combination. I'm surprised to see a sign that touts fishing bait, which is new since I was last home. Mr. Myers prides himself on his specials, so his latest doesn't faze me. In the window hangs a sign that says: Free bag of potato chips when you buy two buckets of minnows.

Near the entrance are three spaces, and I thank my

lucky stars to find one empty. Inside, I stock up on essentials: Ramen and Diet Coke. Along the way, I add in some vegetables and a little meat, though I hesitate to buy anything I might not use in the immediate future. My time in Shaconage has an expiration date.

I'm standing in the produce section, weighing the pros and cons of a white versus red onion, when someone steps into me. The forceful contact pops the onion out of my grip. My fingers try to make purchase and fail and I watch as it slips to the floor.

With a sigh, I bend to grab it when my arm is suddenly wrenched behind me, the force of it jerking me to stand. The shock leaves me breathless as I look at the man holding me, a face I don't recognize. The man before me is thin, but his grip is strong. Dark circles and unkempt hair are his most noticeable features. His face quickly darkens to an angry purple, and with each passing second, his hand tightens around my upper arm.

"You ruined my life." He says it so low I almost don't hear it at all. No matter how hard I wrack my brain for clues as to who he can be, I find no memories of his face.

"I'm sorry," I say as my eyes scan the store for help, my voice calm and placating. "I think you've mistaken me for someone else."

If anything, this enrages him more, and I feel the nails on his fingers dig into my arm. "You bitch. You took everything from me."

"Hey! You're hurting me!" I shout, my voice pitching higher with each word. There isn't an employee in sight, and with each additional second we're alone, it becomes harder and harder to breathe. I pull as hard as I can against his hold, but he doesn't budge. My only option is to give him enough pain to let me go; I'm going to knee him in the crotch. I lift my foot from the floor just as the sound of footsteps registers somewhere behind us.

"Let her go." My breath shudders out of me on a strangled cry of relief at the sound of Ben's voice. The man holding me startles at the sound and drops my arm. Teetering for a moment, I try to catch my balance on my still-lifted leg before lowering it.

As he pivots to face Ben, I notice he has a limp, his movements slightly uneven. "You know she's poison. She ruined my life and yours. She needs to understand, Ben. She needs to pay."

Wait a minute. Do they know each other? Ben says nothing to this, only stares at us both as if waiting for something.

I've had enough. "Who *are* you? I'm pretty sure I'd remember if I ruined your life, and last time I checked, the only life I've ruined is my own." The last part pours out of me before I can reel it back in, and I cringe. Ben gives me a questioning look but, as usual, doesn't comment. My captor, on the other hand, laughs.

"Are you serious? You took my livelihood, and you don't even remember me?" Before I can register he's moved, he lunges toward me with his hands outstretched like claws. I jump back just as Ben wrestles him away. The sound of my heart pulsates thickly in my ears so that I can hardly hear Ben when he tells me to wait as he escorts the man out.

Eyes squeezed tightly shut, I struggle to stay calm. At

first, I try to hold myself upright against the shelf. Massaging my chest above the area of my heart, I remind myself I'm safe over and over again.

Ben finds me right where he left me, only now I'm seated on the floor by the vegetables. He stares at me for a moment, and I do the same from my spot on the floor. The sweat-soaked hair in my eyes has little to do with the summer heat and everything to do with the panic attack I just had—an attack I'm thankful he missed. Taking his offered hand, I pull myself to stand. Briefly, I busy myself with dusting some onion shavings off my pants and avoid his gaze—a necessary distraction as my mind is still reeling.

"Who was that guy?" Ben obviously knows this man. One who thinks I ruined not only his life but also Ben's. An argument can be made for the latter, but certainly not the former.

"Do you really not know?" he asked, arching his brow and setting his mouth in a thin line, giving the impression he doesn't believe it is possible. I shake my head.

"That was Mark Jeffers."

Oh. I pivot toward the door as if I can see him still standing there. Of course, he's not. My shoulders sag, suddenly heavy with an unbearable weight of guilt.

"I didn't recognize him. He looks...different." It's immediately clear that was the wrong thing to say. It's like I can't say or do anything right around Ben.

"Well, that's what happens to a man when he loses everything. You've spent all these years acting as though you're the only one who lost something when Vin died, but let's be clear, Cleo. I lost a brother. My parents lost their son. This town lost a great man. Mark Jeffers? The man who was driving your car that day, who I'm sure you've not thought of once since you left. God. You're so self-centered." He pauses, lips pressed together in an unforgiving line. He takes a deep breath before continuing in a tamer tone. "First of all, he lost his leg in the crash. He lost his business to creditors." Ben pauses again, as if debating if he should share more. He seems to decide to lay it out because he continues without further hesitation. "His wife left him after they lost the house, and then his son died in a robbery after he moved to Knoxville with his mom."

He pushed off the wall when he started talking and, now that he said his piece, stands stiffly in front of me.

I don't know what to say. I'm saddened to hear that Mr. Jeffers' son died, but I don't see how it can be considered my fault.

"Are you being serious right now, Ben? Mr. Jeffers lost his business because he was found to have illicit drugs in his system when the accident occurred. He was negligent. I don't wish him ill will, but the accident that killed Vincent was his fault. Not mine." I do my best to keep my voice quiet and non-confrontational while I speak. "While we're on the subject, I'll just say it. I left because I knew my very existence was harmful to your family's peace of mind. Your mother couldn't look at me. Everywhere I went, I was this nasty little reminder of what was lost."

"Don't feed me that bullshit, Cleo. You didn't even let his body get cold in the ground before you ran off. Hell, you left before the funeral."

He has me there. The core issue this town has with me is that even if they could have accepted that I had gone from dating Ben to marrying Vincent, I still left. And not only did I leave, but I left without saying goodbye or even burying my dead husband. Even though it hurts, I can't give him any further explanation. I made Vincent a promise and after everything, keeping it is the least I can do. Instead, I just nod and look down at my feet. Why does it feel like my heart is being ripped in two? Is it possible that Ben's opinion still matters to me? My pride revolts at the thought, but my heart tells me it's true. It's pathetic.

It takes every ounce of willpower I have to look him in the eye, but somehow, I manage it. "I shouldn't have left how I did. It was wrong of me, and Vincent deserved a better wife than he got. There's not a day that goes by that I don't wish that Vincent had lived instead of me. I can't change the past, but don't think I don't have regrets because I have too many to count." Voice thick with emotion, I don't say more. It's best I don't. I'm likely to embarrass myself by crying in front of him if I say more. He'd probably consider that a manipulation tactic.

He surprises me when he briefly touches my arm; the action startling me. "I don't wish you dead, Cleo. I just wish he were here." His eyes are almost kind, the blue hue mellowed. I start to apologize, but he stops me with a raised palm. "I don't want to fight anymore. Can we call a truce, focus on Dahlia, and let the past stay in the past?"

My throat is raw with unshed tears. It's almost like talking to the Ben I used to know, and it's hard to handle. Nodding, I clear my throat.

"I'd like to talk more about the letters."

7

"Dahlia?" I whisper her name and squeeze her hand, hoping for some small sign of life. I fall back into the chair next to her bed when she shows no reaction to the sound of my voice and I don't know what to do. Netta had gone home hours ago, and I'm all alone here. I feel helpless in a way that I haven't felt since Vincent died.

I've worked so hard to develop my life outside of Shaconage. I'm stronger and more confident now. When I speak, people listen. My art gets mostly praise and positive, glowing reviews at showings, and I sell well. I have wonderful friends, though I'll admit I keep them in the shallows regarding the life I left behind here. I saw a therapist for ten years. My life is good, damn it.

My breath is coming in gasps, and I'm fully sobbing now, snot running down my nose to mix with the tear tracks on my face. I reach for a tissue and blow my nose, the action halting my weeping. My face is sticky wet when I touch it, and I'm sure my nose is cherry red.

If Dahlia were able, she'd run her soft hands through my hair, like she did the day I lost Vincent—and the baby—and tell me I'm strong, and I'll be okay. At the thought of the baby, I rub my abdomen in small circles, remembering the loss—one I don't let myself acknowledge most days.

I remember it all so clearly. Those first anxious days after learning I'd soon be a mother. The fear of raising a child on my own turned to joy and the promise of a forever with Vincent. Just before the wedding, he brought up potential baby names. If it was a girl, he suggested we call her Daphne. For a boy, he liked Samuel. He admitted it was because he wanted to call him Sammy and take him to T-ball. I smile, picturing the day he brought home the little Tennessee Volunteers onesie. It was so small, and I loved the way he held it in his big hands, smiling at it like it was Versace instead of from Target.

Dahlia never blamed me for Vincent's death like everyone else. She never called me a harlot or questioned my motives. She was able to see past my hasty marriage to the truth. Vincent died because of Mark Jeffers' intoxication. It was never my fault. The rest of the town, however, saw me as Vincent's doom. Of course, Vincent and I had told no one we were expecting a child. It was enough of a scandal that we were together, and so soon after my relationship with Ben had ended, that the announcement of a child might have caused even more of an uproar. In the end, we decided to announce the baby after our honeymoon. Then it became only Dahlia and me holding the secret. Now, it seems, it's just me. *When I die, no one alive will know my baby existed.*

After such big losses, I had to leave. Dahlia never yelled at me, never questioned my decision. When I finally called her days later, she comforted me. She sent me money. She simply loved me through it. It's hard being here without her supportive hands holding me up.

Thoughts of the baby and the life that could have been bombard me, racing through my mind like passing cars on a bullet train. There's not a moment to examine one before the next one crashes into me. My chest tightens with each breath, and the edges of my vision blur in and out. I am no stranger to this sensation. It is one my therapist has helped me to navigate many times. As hard as it is, I know I need to get my breathing under control.

Deep breath in, Cleo. Count to five. Let it out. Okay, again. I tell myself this over and over, doing my best to block the memories and instead focus on each individual breath. After what feels like an eternity, it's over. My chest remains sore from the effort of breathing through the tightness, but I'm back in control. A quick glance at my phone tells me I must leave soon if I'm to have any chance of meeting with Ben today. It's time to read the rest of the letters.

8

I text Ben and ask to meet at Dahlia's place. I want to walk the scene with him and look at some of the yearbooks. Maybe he'll see something I'm missing. After all, he was the focal point of my life back then. If someone had been obsessed with me at that point, the photos might help him remember something he's forgotten or even spark something from my own memories.

I get to the house before Ben, but I'm feeling raw and vulnerable after my time with Dahlia. Even if it's only for an hour, I need a distraction. I decide to start by painting the pecan tree in the backyard. Painting helps to calm my mind, and I don't want any lingering sadness from this morning overshadowing this meeting. I need to be focused and in control of my emotions. Ben called a truce, and it's time to let the past go. Plus, I feel like an ass focusing on my drama with Ben when the focus needs to be firmly on finding the person who hurt Dahlia.

I run through a list of suspects in my head as I paint. First, there's the man in the brown truck that Macy saw leaving here recently. It's such a small town, and brown isn't as common as white or silver, so it could be a lead. Second, there's Mark Jeffers. If he can approach me in broad daylight, in town, then what would stop him from hurting Dahlia, defenseless and alone at home?

The letter said the assailant had been *waiting* for me —to be with me—for the last thirteen years. It has to be someone I know, especially on a personal level. Then again, if it is someone I know intimately, that rules out Mr. Jeffers. I only met him once before the accident. It's possible Dahlia's attacker is someone I barely know, or maybe even someone I don't know at all. My heart sinks at the thought.

I hear the sound of tires on gravel and pack away my supplies before carrying the canvas with me around the house and to the front porch, holding it awkwardly away from my body to avoid any transfer of paint to my clothing.

I smile hesitantly when I see Ben standing at the door, a bouquet of pink and red camellias in his hand. Twisting the flowers between his fingers, he frowns at them. He doesn't notice me immediately, giving me a moment to appreciate him. He has broadened since high school yet remains lean and fit. I know part of that is because of his time in the military, and I suspect he's still running every morning the way we did in high school. I hasten my step, small butterflies dancing in my stomach at the sight of him.

At the sound of my canvas clapping against my

knees, his head snaps up. His eyes find me, pausing for a moment on the canvas in my arms before trailing up to my face. He sees my smile and backs up a step before looking down at the flowers. "Cleo, hey, I found these on your step."

Oh. Disappointment zings through me. I do my best to tamp it down. I place the canvas to rest on an old rocking chair and reach for them. He doesn't hand them over. He doesn't so much as look at me. Instead, he stares somewhere just over my head.

What is he doing? "Okay, you can give them to me now." My left hand goes to my hip, and I thrust my other hand toward him once more, palm up. He still hesitates, pulling the bouquet just out of reach.

"What the hell, Ben? Just hand me the flowers." The words hiss out of me, and despite my best efforts, my blood boils. So much for our truce. Is he trying to piss me off?

The glazed look leaves his eyes, and he straightens, shaking his head, finally making eye contact once more. "No, you don't understand. I *can't* give them to you. *There's a note.*" I hear myself audibly inhale at his words, and I yank the flowers from his hand. He doesn't fight me.

The flowers are arranged in a patterned bouquet of pinks and reds with a single white bud at the center. The attached note is written in block lettering on cardstock.

Pretty Camellias for the one I love.

I turn the card over, but there is nothing else. A single line of bullshit. *What the actual fuck?* Without thinking, I hurl the flowers into the yard. They land in an unsatisfying heap at the bottom of the steps. I scream at the top of my lungs because I don't know what else to do. It's as if the world is falling out from under me, and I can't find a foothold.

I run into the yard and pick up the flowers. With shaky hands, I rip the card from the attached twine. I start to tear it in two, but before I can, I feel Ben's hand on my arm. His gentle touch surprises me, and I drop my hands. He gently takes the card from me. He removes a small plastic bag from his backpack and deposits the card inside. Then, surprising me further, he places it on the ground and pulls me into a hug.

9

We sit in silence on the living room floor and study the letters. It appears Dahlia started receiving the letters six months ago. I'm sure she considered them a nuisance at first because, from what I can see, they aren't threatening, only weird.

The first, dated almost exactly six months ago, simply reads:

> Dahlia, it's nearly the anniversary of the accident that took our Cleo away. We all miss her and hope she comes home soon. Thirteen is a lucky number and let's hope this is a sign of good times ahead. - A Friend

I note the phrase "our Cleo" and re-read the letter a couple of times. *Okay.* It does seem to be someone I know or at least someone local. Most of the letters are the same, mentioning the accident or me. The letters continue to reference the anniversary and fate. I make notes in my notebook:

- our Cleo
- anniversary of accident is important
- fate

It's not until the final month of letters that I start to feel dread. Dahlia received three letters last month. They range from pleading to threatening. It's painful to imagine how Dahlia felt as she read each one. I wish she would have told me about them, but then again, I made it clear I wanted no part of anything related to Shaconage. If only she had known that disdain didn't extend to *her*. I copy the letters in my notebook.

Listen, Bitch..
I've tried to be nice, but I'm losing patience. Cleo needs to come home. Make it happen.

Dahlia,
I'm sorry for my last note. You have to understand. I'm just worried about her. Tell her to come home where she can be safe and loved by us. I know you miss her just as much as I do.

Dahlia. I'm done playing nice. Tell Cleo to come home or I'll make her.

My stomach clenches, and the scar on my abdomen

burns as I read the words. Realistically, I know the white-hot stabbing pain I feel is not real, but it's excruciating, nonetheless. This is not new for me. My therapist says reminders of the accident and what I lost can cause these phantom flares. They are a product of my mind, a trauma-reaction, but it doesn't make them any less real in the moment. I focus on my breathing and silently count to five, over and over, until the pain dissipates, and my breaths are even once again.

The cramping in my stomach remains, though manageable; a quick glance at Ben tells me he is unaware of my unraveling. I sigh in relief at such a small mercy.

Returning my attention to the letters, guilt crowds my mind. Who? Who could do this to Dahlia? Better yet, what desperation would lead someone to hurt the only person I have left in this world? And if they will do this to her, what will they do to me once they have me?

I lay photos on the carpet in front of me, turning to Ben to ask him about his progress, but stop to stare at him instead. He is seated across from me, legs crossed under his knees, where he pages through a yearbook. I watch as he flips through the pages, pausing to take notes before continuing.

His dark hair falls across his brow, occasionally pushed back by his impatient and distracted hands. I sit mesmerized by his fingers as he flips the pages or picks up a pen to scrawl across the paper. The hypnosis is interrupted when I realize he has stopped moving. I pull my eyes from his hands to his face. His eyes are glued to the page in front of him. As I watch, the edges of his mouth tighten and crease into a hard line. Curious, I leave my spot and crawl close before plopping next to him in a way that feels way too much like a Cleo that shouldn't exist anymore.

I peer down at the page at a photo of Ben and me, but also of Jenny, Macy, Mark, and Joe. It was a group trip we took to Atlanta our senior year. We're standing in front of the entrance to the Atlanta Braves stadium. Joe and Ben are doing a funny dance, and the rest of us are laughing. I smile at the photo, turning to Ben in delight. My own smile drops at the lack of his.

"What?" I ask because I can't figure out what could possibly be frown-worthy about it. It's a decent photo, and my memory of that day is wonderful.

Ben points a finger at the photo, to Michael. "I wonder where Michael is these days. He used to have a crush on you, remember?"

I laugh out loud at the thought. "Michael is happily married and settled in Tucson."

"Tucson? Isn't that close to where you live now?"

"How do you know where I live?" Ignoring his question, I ask my own, surprise lacing my words. I keep my residence private, not because I fear being found but because I like my privacy. Especially when it comes to those I left in Shaconage.

"I haven't been keeping tabs on you, if that's what worries you. Dahlia told me you were there. She missed you, and I think she thought I might be able to convince you to come home." He shrugs and gives me a small smile.

My heart freefalls at the sight of it directed at me. With little thought, our shoulders touch. I let myself lean against him-just a bit. For the first time since my return, I feel something close to comfort. With a gasp, I sit up, the smile falling away as dread sinks into my gut.

"I think I might know who it is."

IO

Like a film reel, my mind drifts back to that hot summer weekend in Atlanta senior year. I wasn't wrong about Michael. Although Ben remembers his crush on me, I know it was harmless; Michael never acted on it. He respected me, and more than that, he respected the relationship Ben and I had.

Yet this trip was important in a way I had done my best to block, hoping never to remember again. Too much happened that year that my pain seemed to pale in comparison. At least, that's what I told myself in the years after it happened. The simple truth was this: I couldn't bear to face it.

I look at the floor instead of Ben, preparing myself to tell him the story I never wanted to share. No one, not even Dahlia, knew about what happened to me that night. As much as I might want to, I know I can't keep this horrible little secret locked away, forgotten, any longer.

I draw in a shaky breath, and I'm surprised to hear a tiny laugh leave my throat. *Why am I laughing?* Shivers roll down my shoulders and spine as I grapple to control the red-hot thrum of my heart pounding in my ears. I don't want to tell Ben about this shame. *It's too much.* He already hates me over Vincent. How much more can he hate me after this?

I jolt when I feel Ben's fingers brush my arm; he pulls back before he takes my hand in his. I look at it for a moment before I look up at him, into his eyes, and let the words pour out of me.

I clear my throat and ask, "Do you remember Joe's brother? Trevor?"

Ben nods. "Yes, but we didn't go to school with him. He was a few years ahead of us and moved away when he graduated."

"He went to school in Atlanta. He took that photo of us." I motion toward the yearbook and the photo of us all smiling.

Ben looks at the photo again and turns to me. "What's going on, Cleo?"

I focus on how solid his hand is, holding mine. "Do you remember when Trevor offered to take me to see the gallery at the college when the rest of y'all wanted to go to the bar?" I continue, not looking at him, refusing to examine the words I'm saying. "He didn't take me to the gallery. He drove me to an empty parking lot in the middle of nowhere. I didn't know where we were, and I asked him what was going on. He laughed at me. He laughed in my face, and he told me I should know what he wanted—that I was going to give it to him." Blowing out a shaky breath, I laugh, and I hear how bitter it sounds. I wince and press my lips together. *Oh, God. Oh, God.* My hand goes to my stomach, rubbing it in small circles, but it's not enough. Nothing will make this better. *Nothing.*

"Cleo." Ben's soft voice brings tears to my eyes. I shake my head, don't make eye contact, and continue, "He...hurt me. I tried so hard to make him stop, but it wasn't enough. After, he let me out in front of the bar, and I never saw him again. He's a sick fuck, Ben. Then he had the audacity to send me a rose a year later, on the same day. He signed it, so I would know who sent it. That's why I thought this could be him. The flowers on the porch are something I think he'd do." Laughter bubbles up, threatening to spill out, yet even that is too hard. I catch my reflection in the mirror, eyes wide in a white face. *You're losing it, Cleo. Get it together.*

Saying it out loud to Ben made it real again. Before, I pushed the memory and pain into a box in the furthermost parts of my mind and tried to pretend it never happened to me. Would I have ever let myself talk about it if Dahlia hadn't been attacked?

I feel myself drifting, something my therapist calls dissociation. From somewhere else, I watch as I begin to disconnect from my body, tendrils of my mind unfurling and falling like the petals of a rosebud. I hear static, and my thoughts start to fade away gently, almost like waves drifting to sea. There is nothing. I am nothing. I am not here.

Ben squeezes my hand, the action dropping me back into myself. I let myself meet his eyes, ready to see disgust and loathing there. Instead, I'm surprised to see tears in his eyes, which eases something inside of me. And just like that, the dam breaks.

II

Beneath the windowsill, crouched in darkness, Love waits. Breathing hard, it listens as Cleo talks of the past. It watches as she cries, and Ben rubs her back, a comfort that should only have been given by Love. Through the slats of the blinds, Love makes a plan because Love is patient.

12

After last night's revelation, Ben hasn't been in touch. We had only been dating a few weeks when Trevor attacked me in that car. Ben always assumed he was my first sexual partner, and *he was*. I do not associate Trevor's actions with sex or with intimacy, only violence and disgust. If I could only find a way to explain this to Ben. The very thought of starting the conversation seems impossible right now when everything is still so raw. I've imagined so many scenarios of what would happen if I laid all my secrets out in a neat row, to come completely clean with him, but promises I made to Vincent grip me tight. I spin the band in circles on my left hand as I consider the weight of its promise, my thoughts turning to a long-ago winter night.

"Have you talked about this with Ben?" Vincent sits beside me on the front steps, the two of us alone here yet unwilling to venture past the front door. Dahlia is at the

church's annual Christmas dinner fundraiser and won't be home for another hour or two. I called Vincent in a panic, asking him to meet me here. His cologne makes him smell like a god, which is distracting because not only does he smell divine, he looks like a model, especially in that blue sweater rolled to his elbows. The DeMarco boys are equally stunning but couldn't be more different in appearance. Vincent is like the sun, while Bennett shimmers like the stars.

I shake my head. "No. I tried to reach him at the base, but no one will let me speak to him while he's in bootcamp. I'm not family. It doesn't matter though. It's done." I think of the note left on the door after that last fight. He's gone, Cleo. Suck it up, you made your bed. Lie in it.

We sit in silence for a while, mostly because we don't have much to say to one another. Vincent just graduated college, and he's working with his dad. I just graduated high school, I'm an orphan and directionless, not to mention the ex-girlfriend of his brother. It's awkward.

He clears his throat. "What do you think? You and me?" I wonder if it's me he's asking or himself. He slaps his hands on his knees and stands up. He turns to me with a smile, playful. Like a scene from a movie, I watch as he drops to one knee and takes my hand in his. "Cleo Boucher, we don't know each other well, but we find ourselves in possession of a precious gift. I value you as a woman and as the mother of the next generation of DeMarcos. You're strong, beautiful, smart, and a gifted artist I know will go far. I can't think of anyone more suited to spend my life with. Will you honor me by taking my hand and being my wife?"

I stare at his hand holding mine, while my other hand

rests on my flat stomach, the baby not yet visible, but present just the same. I think of the baby, of the future I envision for it, and nod, a small smile on my lips. Vincent pulls me into a tight hug, his lips feather-soft on the crown of my head.

Pounding at the front door sends me to my feet in a rush, scattering my memories. With quick steps, I reach the door and swing it open without thought, expecting Ben, or even Macy, to be on the other side. But it's neither of them. Instead, it's Mariah DeMarco. My very own reluctant mother-in-law has come to pay a call.

My mouth opens wide, but no greeting comes. I force myself to shut it, feeling myself swallow the air that holds me in a chokehold. Without much thought, I step to the side. She shoves past me, sunglasses covering dark hair that's gathered in a tasteful clip at her nape. Mariah is always put together, and today is no exception. Automatically my hand goes to my own hair, catching on to the tangles that are rapidly matting together on top of my head. I wince, remembering I hadn't bothered to brush it this morning, my mind preoccupied with last night's drama.

Before I can offer a greeting or even a beverage, she holds up a hand to silence me. She reaches into her enormous Tory Burch handbag and pulls out a newspaper. Curious, against my better judgment, I take it, opening it to the spotlight article that covers the entire page. My heart lurches upon reading the headline, then breaks in two when I see the photos.

"ANOTHER ONE BITES THE DUST? CLEO BOUCHER DEMARCO RETURNS TO SHACONAGE BUT TO WHAT END?"

Two photos sit beneath this headline. The larger of the two is one I know all too well. My stomach burns when I see the photo, Vincent's body draped across mine, cold and stiff. His soul was long gone at that point. I had held him for at least an hour before they found us. In addition to my other injuries, I suffered from hypothermia. I hadn't felt the cold seeping into my bones, turning my veins to ice.

At first, everyone assumed we were off for a bit of privacy before the reception. After an hour, worry set in, and a few of the guys went back up the mountain to look for us. One such guest, Devin Mathews, took a photo that still haunts my dreams. Mathews was present at the wedding at the request of Vincent's mother. He was meant to cover a society wedding; instead, he made it to the big leagues with that single shot. He made his career off the pain of this family.

I feel my jaw tighten, my teeth beginning to hurt, as I silently read the caption. I tear my eyes away from it to the much smaller photo below. It's one of Ben and me, taken in the front yard of my house. In it, he's holding me close, folding me into an embrace. You can't see our faces, which lends itself to a picture of romantic intimacy and not the comfort of a friend. I scan the article until I find the byline: Devin Mathews. *So he's back too. What a nice little reunion.*

I fold the paper in two and set it on the credenza by the front door. I tell myself to take deep breaths and to be confident. How Mariah Demarco has retained the ability to turn me into a frightened mouse baffles me. I turn from the table and hear the slap before I feel it spread across my face like wildfire. I stumble back, a mix of pain and shock zipping through me. As I teeter and try to catch my balance, I smack into the credenza, grasping the ledge with my left hand. From the corner of my eye, I watch in horror as a photo of my parents and Cecily shatters on the floor. I quickly pick it up, only to see a shard of glass has punctured the face of my mother. I feel a single tear fall, which I wipe away.

When I turn back to Mariah, I see a flash of regret before her face hardens again. White-hot anger rolls through me, and I leap forward before realizing it. *No, I tell myself firmly, don't lower yourself to her level. She is not worth it.* Instead, I veer to the right, making a wide detour around and away from her. I take a slow, deep breath before speaking.

"Mariah. I need you to leave now." I walk toward the kitchen, cradling the photo like a child, my steps large and quick. Soon, all that remains of Dahlia could be a photo like this.

It's hard to comprehend that I'm barely thirty-one, yet I've lost almost everyone I've ever loved. Dahlia is still living, but she might as well be dead. Maybe it's time I admit she's really gone. The ache of the inevitable loss threatens to swallow me whole. I hear footsteps behind me as Mariah follows me into the kitchen. I keep my back to her, hopeful she'll take the hint. She doesn't.

"You can't throw me out! I'm not picking up the pieces of this family when you get a wild hair and run off again. Vincent didn't deserve it. I'll be damned if I let you destroy *everything* we've fought to rebuild since you left." The last word ends with a screech.

She's come close enough to crowd me in the corner of the kitchen counter. Weariness flows through me at her words, filtering into every corner of my soul. Her very presence obliterates the meticulously constructed wall I've erected around myself over the years. "Do you expect me to just quietly sit by while you send another of my sons to an early grave?"

I feel the earth inside of me quake and tumble into rubble with each word she catapults my way. I'm tired of taking the blame for Vincent's death. Even now, Mariah is sure Vincent's death is my fault, despite clear evidence it was the negligence of another that killed him. *Fuck that.* Pulling myself to my full five feet ten inches, I surprise even myself when I hear the ice in my voice.

"If you don't back the fuck up, Mariah, so help me God, you're going to regret coming here. And while you're at it, get the hell out of my house." I don't yell. I don't hit. I simply state facts. If Mariah doesn't leave this property, I'll pull her out by her hair.

We're locked in a stare when a creak in the hardwood startles us both. It's Vince, my father-in-law, and I feel instant relief at his presence. He will take control of the situation and get Mariah out of here. Much like his son,

Vince is pure goodness and light. And just like his son, he chose the wrong woman to commit his life to.

He swallows before giving me a small smile. My throat tightens at the familiarity of it, so like Vincent's smile. Without meaning to, one side of my mouth gives a small one in return. *God, I'm unhinged.* One minute I'm ready to fight, and now I'm smiling. What I need is a good, strong drink and some hot sex to get through this bullshit. I'll have to settle for the bottle of whiskey I saw under the sink earlier. I shake my head at the thought. *Really, Cleo. Sex and whiskey. That's what's on your mind right now?*

I step around Mariah to embrace Vince, my heart settling back into a steady rhythm. It's been so long since my own dad passed that I can't help myself. I let him squeeze me tight, and the wrinkles in my battered heart smooth the rest of the way out when he kisses the top of my head. I pull back and take a long look at his face.

The lines I see there are more pronounced now, and his hair is an attractive gray. It's easy to see Vincent there, in his eyes and jawbone, but also signs of the man Bennett will one day become. I wonder how it feels for them to be reminded that Vincent, who looked so much like his father in life, will not continue to age and take on his father's characteristics. A sigh bubbles up at the thought of their pain, so much like my own yet different too.

Feeling more confident and benevolent with Vince in the room, I turn back to Mariah and take a deep, steadying breath. "I understand that photo was hard for you to see. It's hard for me to see too. I need you to know this: there is nothing romantic nor has there been anything romantic between Ben and me in over thirteen years. The last thing I came back here to do was to start anything with him, to wreck your life further, or even to see you or him. I didn't even know he lived here, for God's sake. I came for Dahlia. It can't be a surprise to you that I came after what happened, and I won't apologize for it." I take a deep breath and continue, "What I will do is apologize for the way I left things. If I could go back and handle things differently, I would, but I can't. You deserve an apology-you both do-and I'm so sorry that I made an already difficult situation worse."

While I spoke, Mariah wrung her hands together, an anxious trait I've seen her do many times. I understand. This is the one meeting I hoped to avoid altogether. When I finish speaking, she blows out a breath and nods in a tight, controlled bob.

Vince is nodding too. "We won't keep you. Our concern led us to make a hasty judgment in coming here. We'll let ourselves out." He has his hand on Mariah's upper arm in a comforting yet authoritative way. It's as if he is reassuring not only me, but Mariah as well, that everything will be fine.

I look at Mariah to see she's staring at my left hand, where I'm absently twisting my band. I look at it now too. To be honest, I rarely look at it anymore, yet I'm always touching it, twisting it over and over throughout my day. Looking at it now, I see a small fleck of blue paint. I stare at the fleck, feeling myself sink into it until blue is the only thing I see.

"You still wear it?" she asks, voice so low I almost

miss it. We make eye contact. I nod and shrug. "He was a great man, and I miss him." It's a simple, yet effective, statement because once I've said it, I see a change in her gaze. It's not a look of love, acceptance, or even forgiveness but, perhaps, one of mutual understanding. Neither of us says another word, and she leaves quietly the way she came.

13

After they leave, I'm at loose ends. I dig my MacBook out of my canary-yellow suitcase and try to open a Google search, only to realize Dahlia has no Wi-Fi. No surprise there. Instead, I open my cellphone browser and enter "Devin Mathews, journalist" before curling up on a wicker couch on the front porch. Cell service is slow, so I set the phone on the cushion beside me and turn my attention to the yard. It's late July, and Dahlia's garden is in full bloom with large trees, flowers, herbs, and vegetables turning an otherwise normal yard into a fairy oasis of color and scent.

The fragrant aroma of herbs and flowers intermingles and tickles my nose with sweetness. If Dahlia were home now, we'd be canning vegetables and making jars of salsa and pickles. No one makes salsa like Dahlia Boucher, and few can resist when it's on the table. Her salsa is hot enough to rival the fires of hell, yet sweet enough to make you forget you were tempting eternal torment. It's no wonder the locals call it Lucifer's Temptation. I start to salivate and make a mental note to pick up some tortilla chips while I'm visiting Dahlia today.

I pick up my cell and note the phone has finished loading various articles with mentions of Devin Mathews. The first one that appears is the *TIME* article featuring the photo of Vincent and me on our wedding day. I scroll quickly past it, unwilling to subject myself to another round of distressing images.

"Devin Mathews wins Pulitzer for his coverage of flooding in Middle Tennessee."

"Devin Mathews invited to White House."

"Devin Mathews wins Congressional Medal of Freedom."

"Embroiled in scandal? Where is Devin Mathews now?"

"Devin Mathews declares bankruptcy. Says no one will hire him."

I click on the articles one by one, skimming praise for his work in journalism. After the photo of us catapulted him to the upper echelons of journalistic stardom, he proved himself further by covering natural and political disasters all over the world, earning him awards and fame.

At some point, he fell out of favor. An affair with a diplomat's wife landed him in some hot water, which was further escalated when his gambling debts were made public. It seems he's made more enemies than just me. I don't know when he moved back to Shaconage, but I know one thing for sure. Devin Mathews is here, and he knows I am, too.

I close the browser and open my contacts, scrolling until I see Tate's name. I hit call, biting my nail as the phone rings on and on. The call clicks as it connects, and I smile when I hear a honeyed voice fill the line.

"Cleo, took you long enough." I can hear his own smile echoing back at me. I feel a blush tickle my cheeks, and I put my hand to my face as if he could see it blossoming there. He's probably sitting at his desk, and I imagine him leaning back in it, feet resting on top and crossed at the ankles. I've seen him do it a hundred times.

"Hey," I say, surprising myself at how shy I sound. We haven't spoken since I left, and I'll admit, this was intentional on my part. I absently touch my lips, thinking of that last meeting.

The Arizona sun was even more oppressive than usual for the start of July. Tate attended my art show, and afterward, we had a late meal at our favorite spot: a hole-in-the-wall diner that specializes in grease. A greasy hamburger was a much-needed distraction after such a poor turnout. We were expecting a much better show. It's certainly true that I've been selling fewer paintings lately, though no overt reason has presented itself.

Tate has been representing me since I sold my first painting nearly a decade ago. He's never steered me wrong, whether that's business related or when choosing the best diners in town. Over burgers and milkshakes, we discussed different methods to revitalize sales. To my dismay, he suggested I create more of an online presence through Twitter and Instagram. At one point, he even suggested I create a TikTok and share my painting process to garner more interest. In theory, it sounds promising, but I'm just not sure I can share such an intimate experience with millions of strangers.

He drove me home afterward, and I watched as we drove past subdivision after subdivision interrupted only by fields of red sand. The contrast between Shaconage and Arizona could not be more different. Dotting the red sand are the cacti, shockingly visible amongst the otherwise barren space.

We ended the night on the back patio, sipping tea and enjoying the slightly cooler temperature evening brings. Sitting side by side on the swing, he put his arm around me and kissed my hair. It felt right. So when he leaned close to touch his lips to mine, I let him. It was sweet and kind. I've been alone for so long that I was surprised to find myself crying. But even then, he was perfect.

In the back of my mind, I've wondered about a possible future with Tate. We are good together. He helps me with investments and the legal side of my business, and our friendship is strong. I spend more time with him than anyone. And when he kissed me, I felt something. And after all these years of stumbling through life numb, it felt incredible. More than that, Tate felt safe. After he left, I lay awake, reliving the night over and over until finally going out to start the day with paint.

Of course, that's when I received the call about Dahlia. And nothing's been quite right since.

I force myself to focus on Tate's words as he goes over details from recent art sales. I'm not exactly worried about money. Still, I have responsibilities to people other than myself now. I take that seriously.

Prior to our wedding, Vincent made me the beneficiary of his life insurance and estate. At first, I felt guilty and even refused to touch the money for several years. After quite a bit of therapy, I used some of it to buy my little house and remodel it with a studio. I still have almost all of it, preferring to use it only when necessary. In the back of my mind, I know he left the money to me because I was pregnant. Now that there is no baby, it makes it hard to accept that it's my money. *Blood money.*

Nearly seven years ago, Tate convinced me to make some investments, and they've been doing well. Because of that, I've started a program to support single mothers called New Hope. I consider it the one good thing I've done with my life, and I like to think Vincent would approve.

I'm curled up on the couch, twirling strands of my hair around my finger while I listen to him go over the stats at New Hope. Recently, one of our youngest mothers graduated from college and has been transitioning out of the program. She recently leased an apartment and secured childcare for her son. Since starting, we've had eighty-three mothers successfully complete the program.

"Okay," he says. "That's it for today. I'll email this over to you when we finish up, and you can let me know if you have any questions." A picture of him clicking away at his keyboard, glasses scrunched up on his face as he focuses on crafting the perfect email comes to me and I smile, imagining his blond curls falling down and over his glasses. How many times have I watched him absently wipe his hair away? I think of what I need to ask him, and my smile fades.

"Tate." I don't know why I stop myself from telling him what I need. Part of me wants to keep him safe from my life in Shaconage. I'm not the same here as I am with him. I'd like to protect that illusion, but I know it's impossible. One way or another, he'll know it all. And he'll either want me or he won't. I clear my throat and start again.

"I need help." As soon as I say it, relief spreads through me like a sigh. He starts to speak, but I barrel on, suddenly eager to tell him about the goings-on in Shaconage.

"Dahlia was attacked; it wasn't an accident. And since I've been here, I've learned some terrible things. We don't know who hurt her, but it's clear she was hurt on purpose. There was a note addressed to me, Tate. *To me.* The Sheriff is investigating, though he doesn't have very many leads. I can't just sit around, though, and I had an idea. I was wondering if you could help me find a private investigator."

Silence greets me on the other end of the line. "Tate?"

"Sorry," he says, "I'm trying to take it all in. What do you mean, the note was addressed to you?"

I tell him the rest of what I know, and I hear him scribbling things down. Adding in the details I found online about Devin Mathews, I ask him to be added to the list. I don't necessarily think Devin hurt Dahlia, but I can't deny it's odd timing that he returned to Shaconage just before Dahlia's troubles began.

"Mark Jeffers made threatening statements to me in the grocery store, and I'm worried he might retaliate in some way. Truthfully, he could be behind Dahlia's attack."

I'm standing on the porch now, having left the couch in favor of pacing out here. I stop and lean my head against the scratchy wooden post by the steps and clear my throat.

"There's one more thing." My chest tightens, and I force myself to remain calm as I make the next request.

"Can you help me find out about the statute of limitations on reporting a sexual assault?"

14

After we hang up, I'm completely wrung out—limp like a wet dishtowel. Familiar hunger aches remind me that I have, yet again, neglected to eat. After rummaging through the meager pile of groceries I've accumulated, I opt to grab a bite at the diner. I grab a pair of sandals and my sunglasses before leaving. On my way to the car, I mentally review the menu in my head, twisting my long, blonde hair into a bun and tucking my not-quite-long enough bangs behind my ears. Everyone warned me I'd regret the bangs. They were right.

I turn out of the driveway, leaving a trail of dust behind me. In the rearview mirror, I catch sight of Macy's Honda Fit and throw up my hand. She continues past Dahlia's and soon catches up to me. She throws on her flashers, so I pull to the side as she does. Within seconds, she is out of the car and running up to my window.

"Hey, girl! I was just headed over to invite you to dinner at the new house." She's bouncing back and forth while she speaks, clearly excited to make the invitation. I want to say yes, but I know I need to see Dahlia. I glance at the clock on the dashboard and calculate the trip. Just enough time if I skip the diner.

"I'm on my way to see Dahlia, but I could come later this evening if 7:30 is okay." Secretly, I'm hoping she'll say no. I'd rather get a sandwich, see Dahlia, and spend the evening doing more research on Mark Jeffers and Devin Mathews. Alone. It's not that I don't want to spend time with Macy, it's more that I don't feel I have the emotional energy to give. Macy, despite being my best friend, drains me. To her credit, doesn't seem put off by the delayed dinner plans.

"Perfect! I planned a casserole, and we can toss that in any time. Just come to my house when you're done. Call the landline if you need me or if something comes up—no cell service up there." She waves her flip phone, and I can't help but smile. Of course, she still has a flip phone. We part ways, and soon I'm headed to Dahlia.

A text from Tate greets me upon my arrival at the ICU. I ignore it and grab an oatmeal cream pie from the vending machine before going into Dahlia's room. I close the door softly behind me as if the smallest sound could wake her. *If only*.

The lights are dimmed, but I don't turn them up. Instead, I slip off my sandals and crawl into the bed with her, snuggling close. I watch the monitor, noting the lines that show her heart keeps beating despite everything else. Right now, that's good enough for me. I just need her heart to hold on long enough for her to wake up. Her hand is small in mine as I clutch it close, slowly smoothing it out like she has done for me in so many moments of stress.

The last time she held my hand like this, I was the one in the bed. Tears well up, and I let them fall. There's no safer place to cry, to remember, than with Dahlia.

Sharp pain slices through me before I've even opened my eyes. A cry of shock pulls me completely awake. I hardly recognize my voice, which sounds muffled and garbled to my ears. I force my eyes open, which feel heavy and thick. Her touch is recognizable before her face, a blur that slowly solidifies before me. I hear her now, whispering to me, as she rubs my hand with her fingers.

"It's okay, Cleo. You're okay, baby." I don't understand where I am and why everything hurts. I concentrate to focus on her face, which looks tired. She's wearing a beautiful purple dress that looks rumpled. Dahlia hates creases. I start to comment but stop when I recognize it as the one she wore to my wedding.

I look down at my dress, but it's not there. A hospital gown has replaced the dress. I jerk to the right, dizziness blurring my vision again at the sudden movement. I close my eyes until it passes and open them again. Taking in the room, dread hits me when I realize where I am.

"Where's my dress?" My throat is dry, sore even, and I desperately want a drink of water. I start to ask for one but don't.

Where is Vincent? He's not in the room. Didn't we just get married? Why can't I remember this? What day is it?

"Dahlia, I—" I gasp and pull my hand from hers to pull at the blankets. I need to see, to check.

No. NO. NOOO. I'm trembling, falling, even though I

know I'm sitting. It's not long before there are more people in the room—doctors, nurses, and orderlies. Right before I fade, I realize I'm screaming.

I jerk awake, feeling raw at the memory. Remembering, I touch my stomach, tracing the scar I now know by heart. The day I woke up was when I lost all remaining faith and hope in the world, in God. Without the baby, I lost my purpose. When I awakened later, I learned Dahlia had gone home to rest, and I was forced to face it alone. In the quiet, I mourned for the baby and for Vincent because I knew, without being told, that he was gone too. He would have been with me if he were living.

I've never remembered the accident. I know I'm lucky to have forgotten but knowing that doesn't make living any easier. The hardest thing to accept is that there is a photo out there that shows I was awake, lucid, for some time after the accident. I had been conscious and able to crawl out of the car, find Vincent, and hold him in my arms. It's all there—the trail of blood from the window to him—on display for the world to see. The dress—once so beautiful—covered in his, mine, and the baby's blood. Sometimes, I wish I had died with them. Yet here I am, living, despite it all.

Stretching, I sit up and glance toward the window to find the sun setting. I kiss Dahlia's brow and close the door quietly behind me.

On the elevator, I open Tate's text.

You might have missed the window to file charges against Mr. Jenkins, but you can still file a report of sexual assault. At some point, your report may help strengthen someone else's case. I know it's not what you wanted to hear, but it's something. Let me know how you want to proceed.

I respond immediately.

Yes, send me the contact info.

And thanks Tate. <3

I hesitate before hitting send. I don't know why I added the heart emoji. It's so out of character for our relationship, for me. Then again, the kiss was out of the norm, too. I hit send before I can think about it too deeply and shove the phone deeper into my pocket, anxious about his response but too anxious to open his quick reply.

A second chime tells me I've received an email. I pull my phone from my pocket and open it to see it's the number of an investigator in Atlanta. I'm busy saving it when I collide with someone. Strong arms catch me, and I squeak when I recognize them. Ben.

"Hi." I'm breathless, and I frown at my reaction. Why am I like this with him? I clear my throat and pull myself up and out of his arms. He smiles at me, and I want to disappear into the floor at the heat that fills my cheeks.

"Been up with Miss Dahlia?" He nods toward the hospital. He's not in uniform this evening, opting for jeans and a plain black tee. I can't help but notice how it compliments his tanned skin.

"Just leaving. I have dinner with Macy in an hour." I start toward the Jeep, and he follows me as he continues to talk.

"You and Macy are hanging out again?"

"Why wouldn't we?" Of course, we're hanging out. If I'm in Shaconage, Macy is close by. It's just how we are.

He shrugs. "You're just...different. You don't really need Macy like you did when we were kids. Macy was always in charge back then. You seem able to speak for yourself these days." He ends the last bit with a chuckle and a shake of the head.

Huh. I guess he's right. Macy did make all the decisions back then. Her personality was bright and bossy— a lot like my sister's had been. Sometimes I wonder if I subconsciously used her as a substitute for that missing piece of me.

Macy had been in charge all right. At least, that is, until I met Ben. She disapproved of that relationship and had no problem voicing it. It was the one time I ever disagreed with her. We didn't talk for months. Eventually, she came around and even supported me through the break-up. In the end, she was right. I couldn't fault her for that.

"You act like I was a pushover, Ben. I recall dating you against all reason and advice. Although maybe I should have taken that advice." I say the last part with a laugh, but he doesn't join me. I turn to find he's stopped behind me. His easy smile, gone. *Damn.*

"Just when I think we're getting somewhere, I

remember it's impossible for us. Goodnight, Cleo." With that, he turns around and walks back toward the hospital, leaving me feeling empty and alone.

I crawl into the Jeep and close the door. I rest my head on the steering wheel. *What a stupid thing to do.* Since we called a truce, Ben has been friendly. He comforted me and didn't judge me when I told him about Trevor. If anything, I'm the one who continues to be an ass.

With a sigh, I pull my phone out and check my messages. At the top sits Tate's text. The one I ignored earlier. In for a penny, in for a pound. I click it, my throat suddenly tight.

;)

Another text follows with a promise to check in tomorrow.

I smile, place the phone in a cupholder, put the car in reverse, and turn toward Shaconage. *God. I hope it's not a green bean casserole.*

It's not green bean casserole, but I can't exactly say it's any better. The soppy mess on the table before me is supposed to be an enchilada casserole.

Macy and I have been staring at it for at least five minutes, neither of us brave enough to try it. It seems Macy's skill in the kitchen remains unchanged since high school. I feel nauseous just thinking of the bout of food poisoning we suffered senior year when she tried her hand at chicken tacos.

I catch her eye, and we both laugh. I push the dish toward her on the table in a "you first" gesture, which sends us both into a fit of giggles that lasts way too long. It feels good to laugh.

"Okay, okay," Macy says and stands. She crosses the room to a cabinet against the wall and pulls a couple of wine glasses from inside. Crossing to the refrigerator, she retrieves a bottle of our favorite wine, pouring us each a glass before returning to rummage in the refrigerator once more. I snort when she returns with two yogurts and a block of cheese.

"Are those even in date?" I ask with a furrowed brow and earn myself a smack on the shoulder. I'm half joking. There's no telling what could be in there. I shake my head and pop the lid on the yogurt, which I'm practically salivating over. It hasn't been a good food day for me. Cream pies and yogurt...a teenager's diet.

I take a sip of my wine, which tastes surprisingly okay paired with the yogurt, and take in Macy's kitchen. It's the only room I've been in so far. Having arrived fifteen minutes late to dinner, we immediately pulled out the failed casserole. I barely had time to take a cursory glance at its contents before we sat down at the table.

The house is partially remodeled with new cabinetry and appliances. The linoleum of the kitchen floor hasn't been touched and reminds me of the odd colors of the 1970s—browns and greens in geometric patterns.

The floor plan is open, so I can see through the living

room, which is decorated in tasteful linens. I hadn't pegged Macy as one who would follow the current trends, but her living room is decorated in the current farmhouse style. Beautiful photos cover the walls in thick frames.

I leave the table, and carrying my yogurt with me, study the photos—St. Augustine, New York City, Yellowstone, Mardi Gras—all of which are beautifully captured. A signature at the bottom reads "Macy Miller."

"Wow, I didn't know you were a photographer! These are beautiful, Mace."

"Hardly a photographer, but thank you, nonetheless. It's a fun hobby, and landscapes are easier to photograph than people. Don't expect me to open a business taking maternity and wedding photos." I laugh at that. Macy has little patience with disorder. I can't imagine she'd do well wrangling toddlers for family photos.

"How many photos are here?" There must be dozens lining the walls.

Macy shrugs. "At least fifty. I've been to every state and some a few times."

I'm impressed. When I left Shaconage, Macy had only been to North Carolina and Georgia on brief trips with friends. Like my family, the Millers didn't venture far from Tennessee. I assumed Macy would be the same, but it seems I'm not the only one who's changed.

There are no photos of family or friends on the walls nor the mantle above the fireplace. A quick look around the room shows no personal photos at all. Macy watches me as I poke into all the nooks and crannies of her perfect living room, an indulgent smile on her face.

"What?" I say, mimicking her smile involuntarily. It annoys me how easily I fall into "twin" mode with her. A dozen years apart, and I'm still a cookie-cutter version of her.

"You're as nosy as ever, Cleo. It cracks me up. Do you remember when we were kids, and you would watch those true crime TV shows? You were convinced everyone in town had sinister intentions."

"To be fair, they were wildly popular in the early 2000s."

"Do you even watch tv anymore? It wouldn't surprise me to hear you are completely cut off from civilization in the desert considering your current online footprint or, rather, lack thereof."

I don't bother to turn around; the unspoken questions in her tone are clear enough. How do you explain to your oldest friend that there are secrets you've never shared, a lifetime lived and forgotten in a mere decade? Answer: You don't.

"The art takes up most of my time, so I've never given it much thought. Although Tate has told me I need to market on social media, so you may see me there soon enough."

"Tate?"

I hear the disapproval in her tone. Ugh. Deep breaths, Cleo. Something about this place, this town, makes me want to hide the important people and things in my life, like Tate. If I can be honest with anyone here, it should be Macy.

"Tate is my attorney and advisor, but more importantly, he's my closest friend in Phoenix. He thinks I need to be more present online to keep sales up. Apparently, my popularity has tanked. Okay, not *tanked*, but there are other artists who are doing their painting live and engaging with fans every day. Just thinking about it is exhausting, and I haven't even started it." I've been avoiding eye contact with her while talking, which somehow made sharing a tiny piece of my life more palatable. I wish it weren't like ripping pieces of my soul to share.

Tate is different from anyone else. Almost immediately, I knew he was solid, that I could tell him everything and anything without fear of rejection or ridicule. I haven't told him about the baby, but he knows I'm widowed. I'm not worried about the rest. If and when I tell him, I know nothing will change.

Funnily, I don't feel that way with Macy or Ben. Somehow I've always felt their friendship and acceptance was tenuous, though I don't suppose Macy has ever given me any true reason to feel that way. Ben, on the other hand, proved this to be true years ago.

"Why do you do that?" I startle, unsure how long I have been thinking about the past and the present intermingling.

"Do what?" I feel my brow furrow in confusion, then realization, when Macy points to where my hand rests on my stomach. Oh. I am not ready for this conversation, but I don't want to brush her off yet again. Better to share something, even if I can't talk about the full scope of my loss.

"It's a habit of mine now, when I'm thinking or worrying. I don't know why I do it, but I massage my stomach over the injury I received during the accident." I give a one-shoulder shrug as though it's not a big deal.

A chirp alerts me of a text message, providing a reprieve from conversation. I pull it out to find a message from Tate.

> My guy says Trevor has been in Shaconage as recently as May.

> He comes often. Records trace calls to Dahlia's house.

> Do you know anything about this?

> Call me.

Why hasn't Ben mentioned that Trevor's been in town? Surely as sheriff of such a small place, he would know of any visitors—especially someone as locally popular as Trevor once was–condescending to visit again. I immediately text Ben, then respond to Tate.

> Wasn't aware.

> I don't understand why he'd call Dahlia.

> Do you think it's connected? Need to know where he was when she was attacked.

> I'll call you in a bit.

> Thanks, Tate.

I put the phone back in my pocket and smooth my hands down my thighs. One. Two. Three times. When I look up again, Macy has her arms crossed, and she looks pissed.

"So was that Ben, or was it Tate?" Her words drip like acid, and I'm shocked at the bite in them.

"Why does it matter?" I notice my own arms are now crossed, and I drop them to my sides, annoyed that I'm, once again, mirroring her.

"You've been gone, what, at least twelve years? But as soon as you get back, you're once again wrapped up in Ben. You tell me you have this close *friend* in Phoenix, but he sounds like another Ben. Honestly, I thought maybe you were over the need to be wanted by some guy all the time, but I guess I was wrong to think it possible. You're *exactly* the same, following some guy around—or two in this case—hoping he'll notice you."

I'm shocked, and I'm pissed. I'm not moping after anyone.

"Okay. That's just about enough, Macy. Of all people, I expected less judgment and more understanding from you. For God's sake, Dahlia has been hurt. Ben and I are talking all the time because we're worried about her, and I'm helping with the case as best I can. It's not romantic, and you know what? Fuck you for even suggesting I'd be running after a guy while she's lying in a hospital bed." My heart is beating faster than the wings of a humming-bird, but I don't care. This is possibly the first time I've ever stood up to Macy. It feels damn good.

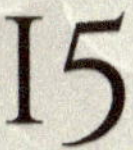

15

After leaving Macy, I'm feeling buzzed and restless. The thought of going back to an empty house is unbearable. I pass by the little farmhouse and continue until I'm leaving Shaconage behind. The roads are cloaked in darkness now, and I'm forced to squint as I glide around bend after bend with only headlights to guide me through the thick fog. I can't help the anxiety that washes over me.

My family died on a night like this. I was at my first sleepover when it happened. My parents and grandparents were on their way home from Cecily's first ballet recital out of town. There was nothing that could be done for them after they hit that bear. When I was a teenager, I went to the library and read the story in the paper. The only comfort is they all died instantly. No one lingered.

The drive passes quickly; my neck is stiff and my fingers white when I finally arrive at the hospital. Night driving never fails to make me anxious, and tonight is no different. The quiet buzz of the engine comforts me as I sit frozen in my seat, finger hovering over the off button. Every time I go inside, I see just how fragile Dahlia really is and how little time I have left with her. Seeing her like that once today was hard enough.

A sigh escapes, startling me in the quiet, and I avert my eyes from the glare of the hospital lights. The jittery energy that brought me here is gone, and I'm left with a body that feels too heavy to hold up. I rub my palm across my chest over and over as I identify the cause of the heaviness I feel there. *Heartache.*

I turn the car off and dig my earbuds out of my satchel, tossing the case back into the bag with a soft click. I scroll through my music until I find a playlist that feels right. The parking lot is almost completely empty with only a couple of cars to keep me company. I'm illu-minated beneath a pole that says "C3." With one more look around the lot to make sure I'm truly alone, I recline the driver's seat until I'm almost completely horizontal with the backseat and close my eyes.

Tapping on the window wakes me. When I open my eyes, I'm greeted by the glare of both the sun and a police officer. Lana Del Rey croons at me from my headphones as I peer through sleepy eyes at the dashboard. I slept for six hours. Of course, I get the best sleep in my car instead of at home in my bed. A series of sharp raps draws my attention back to the officer, who motions for me to roll down the window.

I put what I think is a friendly smile on my face as I start the car and roll it down.

"Hello." I fight not to roll my eyes at how sugary-sweet my voice sounds and keep the smile firmly in place. "I came to visit my grandmother but must have nodded off in the car. It was a little too early when I arrived and must have fallen asleep." My shoulders roll in a helpless gesture.

"That's fine, ma'am," he drawls as he leans down into my window with a smile of his own, "but you'll need to go inside now or leave the premises." I watch as he scans the car, and I wonder if I look like I'm sleeping off a few drinks. A glance in the driver's mirror says yes, I look like I've had one too many. *Maybe more than a few.* My hand goes to my hair instinctively, but I drop it quickly. What's the point, really?

Instead of explaining further, I nod and reach over to grab my satchel, rolling up the window and turning off the car. After he takes a step back, I open the door and step out. I pull my hair into a messy bun, wave goodbye, and head inside.

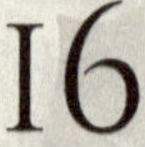

16

I'm lying beside Dahlia when Ben's number comes across the screen. I catch myself throwing a glance at her before answering the phone with a sigh. She would have more than a few opinions about Ben and me being chatty. Whether those thoughts would be positive or negative isn't exactly clear. Naturally, after our history, I assume she'd feel negative about it but, from all accounts, Dahlia and Ben have continued to have a good relationship. I'm both confused and intrigued by it. Ben said Dahlia kept him up to date on my comings and goings in Arizona. Why did Dahlia do it? And why did Ben care?

I clear my throat before speaking, but the words still come out huskier than I'd like. "Hey, what's up?" I pick at a frayed piece of the blanket, phone tucked under my chin.

"Cleo, oh my god. Where are you?" His breath is hitched, and the crunch of gravel echoes under his boots with each increase in his step. I drop the blanket and sit straight up in the bed.

"What is it? What's wrong?" The beat of my heart is loud in my ears, and bile begins to inch its way up my throat. *Damn acid reflux.* I swing my legs over the side of the bed, trying to keep it at bay.

"Where are you?" Something in his voice tells me nothing is okay.

"With Dahlia. I've been at the hospital all night. Well, basically. What's going on?" I stand up, walking to the window to peer out at the street below, looking for monsters in the shadows.

"Stay with Dahlia. I'll be there as soon as I can. Don't leave. Don't come home. We need to talk. *Promise me.*"

A look at my bag on the table shows my keys peeking out of the corner. I turn to Dahlia, so small in the bed, and sigh. I'm so damn tired of sighs.

"I'll be here but make it quick." I hang up without another word and try to lie back down next to Dahlia. The acid reflux has me up in seconds, and I massage my throat as my anxiety increases. I retrieve my bag and pull out a bottle of Xanax. I study it as I try to talk myself out of a panic attack. My hands are shaking, and I try three times to unscrew the lid. I give a little huff before taking a deep breath and trying again. Eventually, I'm able to open the bottle and pour out a single white pill and toss the bottle back in the bag. The water is tepid as it slides down my throat, carrying its cargo down to soothe the quivering in my gut.

I pace in a small square around the room, carefully avoiding Dahlia's bed and equipment. After what feels like a hundred laps, I surprise myself when I let out a shriek and stamp my foot. *Fuck this.* With decisive steps, I grab my things, hurrying to the door. I open it only to be greeted by the officer I met earlier in the parking lot.

"Oh." He smiles at me and holds out a hand. I take it without thought.

"I'm Nick. Got a call from Ben over in Shaconage. He said to keep an eye on you and your granny 'til he gets here." He's still standing in the door frame, blocking my exit.

"Am I a prisoner...Nick, was it?" I indicate his position and motion for him to enter the room. He hesitates and then steps inside, closing the door behind him.

"Of course not, Ms. Boucher. But if Ben believes you need watchin' over then I want to make sure both you and your granny are taken care of. Which means I need you to cooperate by staying here with me."

His tone is placating, but instead of soothing me, it scalds like censure. I want to argue, storm out, and tell him to get lost, but he has a point. If I leave, and he follows me, who will watch over Dahlia? I nod and take up a position by the window, watching for Ben's truck. I steadily chew away the last remnants of fingernail polish on my thumb while I watch and wait.

Nick sits in a chair by the door, scrolling on his phone. Muted static and voices come and go from the radio on his hip. He ignores it, continuing to tap away on his phone as the minutes pass. Nick clears his throat, and I realize I've been staring at him. He smiles but says nothing. I know my face is red, so I turn back to the window and study the passersby.

After an eternity, Ben pushes through the door, and I watch as Nick slips out without a word to either of us. With quick strides, Ben reaches me and crushes me to him. I feel his lips on my hair. I can't help but close my eyes as I breathe him in. He holds me for less than a minute before letting me go.

I step back but wait for him to speak first. He's a mess. The careful look of self-control he seems to always wear has slipped; I can see it in his eyes. Something has deeply upset him. He glances at Dahlia before motioning for me to take a seat. I hover on the edge of the bed as he takes one of the empty chairs in the room. He clears his throat and then takes my hand.

"I'm sorry I freaked out on the phone earlier. It's just...I didn't know where you were, and when I got the call, I feared the worst."

"What call, Ben?"

He squeezes my hand in his and rubs his thumb against mine. "This morning, I got a call that there was a break-in at your house; there was a lot of blood at the scene. I thought—you weren't home—it was..." He glances away from me, searching for words his vocabulary lacked the depth to say. I barely take note of it, my mind circling back to one single word.

"Blood?"

17

It's overcast and dreary, fog smothering the spaces between trees and water. The forty-minute drive back from the hospital took over an hour in the dense haze. More on instinct than with any visibility, I turn into the little gravel driveway and park just in front of the steps. Ugly yellow tape has been stretched across the two pillars. The word "caution" covers the now-faded sharpie I swear I can still smell.

Feeling drained, I pull myself out of the car and walk over to it, remembering how meticulously Dahlia measured my height every year as a child. I run my fingers over the barely visible "7" and dip under the tape to take the stairs two at a time. The screen squeaks as I enter, despair washing over me. The one place that's always felt so safe now feels sterile and eerie.

A creak from another room startles me, and I realize I've been holding the doorknob in my hand. How long I've remained in the doorway is unclear to me. Seconds or minutes, I'm not sure.

The sound of footsteps in the kitchen sends my heart into my throat, but I can't make my feet move. My gaze is frozen, staring straight ahead at the connecting doorway. The only sound in the room is my breath, puffing in and out through my nostrils, the frequency increasing with each moment that passes.

When headlights hit a deer, they freeze. No matter how far away you are from them, they don't move. Their eyes remain wide, their head turned slightly toward the beams. If the driver can't swerve fast enough or, in some cases, doesn't see the deer at all, they die. Horribly. Painfully. And if they don't die with the first hit, the only humane thing to do is to put them down.

Like a deer, I can't move. I'm frozen, waiting for the kill shot.

The door swings open slowly, and before I can die of a heart attack, a soft hum evaporates my fear like a soft hand smoothing out a wrinkled bed sheet. I sag in the doorway, glad to be still holding the doorknob. It's the only thing holding me up.

Netta, in all her five-foot glory, stops with a gasp. "Oh, my word. Goodness child, you gave me a fright." Her small hand rests just above her heart, and her eyes are so wide, I'm suddenly worried she might have one.

I laugh, partially at the absurdity of the situation, but also to lighten the mood. With a decisive nod, I rub my hands down my shorts and give Netta a smile. This is still home, and I won't be afraid here. At least, not today. I walk over to Netta, murmuring a half-joking apology and wrap her in a big hug, my extra ten inches in height dwarfing her. I breathe her in, finding comfort in the smell of peppermint and lavender.

Over her head, my gaze drifts toward my bedroom and what awaits me there. I step back from Netta and smile down at her. Knowing me all too well, she shakes her head with a sigh.

"You won't find anything there. It's been handled." I look at her hands, and she laughs. "No, I didn't scrub anything. Ben had a crew come in and take care of it. Though you won't be able to sleep there tonight. You might want to consider sleeping at Macy's or in Dahlia's room. Personally, I'd feel better if you slept somewhere else." She shrugs when I start down the hall and returns to the kitchen.

The door is opened wide, and I step over the threshold, more curious than anything. My bedspread is no longer draped across my bed, and I make a note to text Ben. Nan made it for me, and if salvageable, I want it back. It's one of the few things I have left of her. It's not just the comforter that's missing, though. My bed is completely bare but, thankfully, blood free.

There wasn't much of me left in the house, to begin with; other than the quilt, there's nothing I'll particularly miss. With a gasp, I turn quickly, searching for my oversized suitcase. It's tucked into a corner of the open closet door, and I lunge for it, saying a silent prayer. My fingers tremble as I pull the zipper open, the sound piercing the quiet. Once done, I flip it open and gasp.

My paintings are gone.

I spend the next hour frantically emptying drawers and flipping cushions. In addition to my paintings, items lost include my mother's locket and my address book. The only items of any monetary value are the paintings. Massaging my throat, my mind drifts to the last time I saw the necklace on Mom. The night of the accident, I begged to wear it to my sleepover. To a small girl of five, it was the most beautiful piece of jewelry in the world.

Perhaps my adoration was influenced by the fact that she never took it off. Simple in design, it was clearly her most treasured possession, above even her engagement ring. When she was just seventeen, my father gave it to her when he told her he loved her. I've heard the story enough times to imagine the necklace held some magic. And perhaps it did. That night, she relented and fastened it around my neck with a kiss on my brow. I never saw her again.

The theft of my address book is puzzling but not overly concerning. All the addresses were recently backed up on the cloud, and I don't truly need the physical copy for any real reason. I carry it out of habit. There are no secret passcodes in its depths, and it isn't a diary, though it's possible the thief had mistaken it for such when they snatched it. The necklace, though cheap in value, was truly lovely. Of course, I'm robbed on the first day that I took it off in a year.

At a much slower pace, every item is slowly tucked back into its place. As I place the last cushion on the couch and smooth the crocheted blanket across the back, my mind keeps returning to the locket and all the people I've lost.

18

It doesn't take long to find a number for the appropriate detective, and as I hit send, I consider my options. Realistically, I'm aware this won't make much difference in my case. But the hope that it could be the key to charges against Trevor in someone else's had me sitting down to make the call.

I'm not sure why, but losing my items capitulated me into action in a way I hadn't expected. As if a dam had broken, the need to do something has me searching for the appropriate precinct to put Trevor behind me for good.

"Atlanta Police Department Communications, how can I help?" a nasally voice drawls on the other end of the line.

It takes only a moment to be transferred to the right department. Hesitantly, I explain my situation and my goal in reporting so many years later.

"Do you have any witnesses or anyone who can testify you'd told them about the assault when it happened?" The detective seems less skeptical than weary when he asks.

"No." I never planned to tell anyone at all. I'm still wrestling with myself at having revealed it to Ben, and in turn, Tate. Though telling Tate had been easier somehow. Tate, I knew, would never judge me or question my word. After everything that's happened, can I really say the same of Ben?

"No, sir, I didn't tell anyone. I didn't plan on reporting at all. But things in my life are different now, and it's just something I need to do. I'm not trying to press charges. I just want it on the record. A record of report." I breathe in and out through my nose shakily as I hear the detective exhale on a long sigh.

"Okay, sure, we can do that. When can you come down to file the report in person?"

"Oh. In person?" I look around the house, a place I no longer feel fully safe, and decide. "I can be there tomorrow morning."

After discussing a few more details, I hang up and walk to the kitchen to ask Netta to check in on Dahlia while I'm gone.

19

Where is she? Love has been watching the house for the last two days, but Cleo hasn't returned. After the first night and day melted into the next, Love slept in her bed. The sweet smell of her perfume clung to her pillow and reminded Love of summer. Love removed the case before leaving the house, replacing it with a clean one.

Last summer, Love watched Cleo paint in her tiny backyard in Arizona. This summer, she is finally home. Home to be loved. Home to be adored and cared for. Soon, she'd see. There is nothing Love won't do for Cleo. Love is kind.

20

I'm exhausted when I pull up at the house, but relieved to have the trip to Atlanta behind me. The detective was kind—kinder than I expected. The report was thorough. As thorough as a report about a crime from nearly twenty years ago can be, I suppose.

When I asked the detective if Trevor had been involved in any cases with other women in Atlanta, all he could tell me was there is nothing pending against Trevor in any of the databases. I guess I should feel relieved but part of me isn't. I can't help but wonder why he chose to hurt me and no one else. Dahlia and I had known Trevor my whole life. He was an adult, nearly twenty-two, when he raped me. I was just a child.

It's likely I will never know why he did it, but I know one thing. I'm done blaming myself. I'll never blame myself again.

Netta called at lunchtime with reports that Dahlia's condition was unchanged. Despite my protests, she offered to stay overnight again tonight. Instead of spending the day with my granny, I spent it deep cleaning the kitchen.

Thankfully, I remembered to charge my headphones on the drive back to Tennessee. I spent the last couple of hours listening to my favorite podcast and have moved on to what I like to think of as my "Get Shit Done" playlist. Currently half inside, I'm scrubbing the interior of the oven as if the survival of the human race depends on how clean I can get it.

I'm humming and swaying to yet another Ed Sheeran song when I feel the touch of someone's hand on my shoulder. Before I can process the familiarity of the touch, I'm a madwoman in action. The oven scrubber connects with the side of Ben's horrified face at the exact moment I realize he's not a threat.

He stumbles back a step with a grunt. "Damn it, Cleo!"

Feeling like an absolute ass, I'm on my feet just as quickly, brush still in hand, though no longer lifted in defense. I step forward and take his face in my hands.

"Hold still," I say as I inspect the damage. Upon further inspection, I can see the bristles of the scrubber nicked the skin, leaving slight cuts interspersed among the welts. Lips pressed together, I look into his eyes. The temporary anger I saw when I hit him was gone as quickly as it came. Instead, he's looking back at me with a comforting and steady gaze. I'm the first to break eye contact, removing my hands and stepping back. Quickly, I cross to a cabinet and remove Neosporin and take out a Band-Aid. I rummage in the first aid kit and find a small box of alcohol swabs.

I lay out my supplies on the counter, opening the swab and bandage and turn to Ben, who walked over while I was looking for supplies. I make quick work of it, cleaning the cuts and smoothing the ointment across his cheek. A smirk crosses my face as I apply a hot pink Band-Aid on a sharp cheekbone. I rub my fingers across it, unable to stop myself from making contact.

He sucks in a breath at my touch; its gentleness surprises me. Curious, I sneak a peek at him, and the look in his eyes has me taking a step back, my hand leaving his face. Before I can move away completely, he stops me, his hand snagging my wrist as I step away. For a moment, neither of us moves, my eyes on his hand, lightly encircling my wrist. I can feel his eyes on me, and a feeling old and forgotten stirs, threatening to send tears to my eyes.

Unable to avoid his stare any longer, I lift my head and let the force of his gaze engulf me. I know this Ben. Butterflies I thought had died take flight, yet I remain frozen to the spot, watching his face in fascination. With hesitation and questions in his eyes, he steps forward. I force myself to keep my face neutral, my feet planted. Standing still proves impossible, though, as he backs me quickly into the corner of the countertop. I glance behind me at the crumbled Band-Aid wrapper before looking back at him. For a moment, we simply look at one another, neither daring to move. With a sigh, he releases my wrist, only to take my face in his hands.

I have only seconds to savor the feel of warm, calloused hands cradling my cheeks before his lips meet mine.

21

Countless tummy aches as a child taught me a long time ago that what tastes good isn't always good for you. So, with great reluctance, I move my hands to Ben's chest and give a small push, ending the sweetest kiss I've ever had.

He continues to hold me but doesn't try to kiss me again. I'm confused, worried even, about this sudden change in him. The kiss was a mistake, and it's obvious it can't happen again, but what's even more of a puzzle is that it happened at all. Clearing my throat, I wait for him to pull away before asking, "Uh, what brings you here?" Nervously, I pick at the hem of my shirt, avoiding his gaze, and feel my cheeks go hot.

With a sigh, he slides farther away before walking to the window. He stares out at the backyard, his gaze fixed on some unknown spot in the darkened woods. Finally, he turns to me, and I see the walls are back up, shuttering his gaze.

"Where were you?" he asks, avoiding my question. I

consider volleying with another question of my own, but instead, I hear myself telling him about Atlanta. When I've finished, I see his shoulders are relaxed, but his gaze is sharp and searching.

"You should have told me, Cleo. I would have gone with you."

I shrug. "I can handle it."

"You shouldn't have to handle it yourself. Damn it, Cleo. Why won't you let anyone fucking love you?" The words are explosive, and I instinctively jump as they echo in the quiet kitchen. I begin to give a snarky reply about love, but stop at the sight of him.

He's pacing, walking back and forth across the small kitchen, his hands in his hair, fingers running across his brow as he speaks with words that are jumbled and fast. Instead of commenting at all, I listen.

"Yesterday, I came by. We found the brown truck. I came here to tell you, but you were gone. Your phone was off when I called." He stops his circuit, throwing his arms in the air. Fascinated, I watch him as he continues, occasionally using his hands to express his point.

"I called Macy, but apparently, you haven't spoken in days. A fact, I'll add, you failed to mention during any of our recent talks. What was I supposed to think, Cleo? You could have been dead." The last was said in a whisper, and guilt hits me like a tidal wave.

"Ben, stop. I'm sorry I worried you. You're right, I should have told you I'd gone out of town." I keep my distance—afraid I'll pull him into my arms if I get too close.

"Why did you turn off your phone?"

"I don't know. I guess I needed to separate my real life from what I was there to do. That was a mistake, I realize that now. I told Netta, but I honestly didn't think anyone else cared where I was."

If he yelled again, I wouldn't be surprised, wouldn't blink an eye. Instead, it is the gentleness in his voice that brings tears to my eyes.

"Why, Cleo? Why do you push everyone away?" His voice is hoarse and strained, piercing my heart like the sharp tip of an ice pick.

"Because everyone leaves." My voice is a whisper when I find the ability to speak. And it's true. Everyone I've ever loved has left me in the end. Soon, Dahlia will be gone, her body already a shell of who she once was.

There's pain in the stare he gives me, but he doesn't deny my words. He knows that he, too, left me behind. I can see the memory of our last night reflected in his eyes.

I had walked out of the house before Ben, wanting to distance myself from the scene inside. Ben's mom went on a rampage when she learned her youngest son decided to forego college in the fall. Not only had he decided to throw away his football scholarship, but he had no other plans lined up. When his parents learned this over a family dinner that Ben brought me to unin-vited, his mom pointed her finger in my face and accused me of influencing Ben to give up his future, to stay home and marry young.

I didn't defend myself, didn't have the chance to. Ben had taken the bait and shamelessly used me in his family war. He flaunted our relationship in their faces, accusing them of being snobs. He didn't deny it when they suggested I was making him stay in Shaconage. Truthfully, I voiced my own concern about his decision to throw away his scholarship, but his parents didn't know that.

Feeling awkward and out of place, I gathered my things and left, standing alone on the porch. Eventually, Vincent came out to stand with me.

"They're really not that bad." Despite his light words, I could tell he was embarrassed, so I gave a small nod and tried to smile. A smile that faded when I heard his mother refer to me as "that bitch," causing a frown to form on Vincent's perfect face. He apologized and returned inside, where I could hear him intercede on Ben's behalf. After a few more tense moments, the screen door smashed into the side of the house as Ben stormed out, passing by without a glance in my direction.

Hurriedly, I followed, barely closing the truck's door before Ben peeled out of the drive. Tires squealing, he turned the radio all the way up and didn't meet my gaze. He was going too fast, careening around curve after curve, sending me into panic mode.

The memory pulls me in, forcing me to relive it.

Thick fog and an inky black sky are the only things I can see. The sound of my heartbeat roars in my ears, and I pull my seatbelt tighter, both hands gripping the ceiling handle to stay upright with each bend of the road.

"Ben, slow down!" My voice screeches above the music, but he doesn't look at me or reply. His bright blue eyes swirl like a raging storm.

"Ben, stop it. You're scaring me!" I'm screaming now, fear

clawing its way up my throat. Why is he doing this? He knows my family died on a night like this.

He takes a curve without braking or slowing, and I close my eyes, scared to see how close we are to the edge and the river below. Around the next curve, Ben jerks the wheel, and I lose my grip on the handle, falling into him with a small scream. I open my eyes to see us miss an oncoming truck by a hair. As we pass, the driver lays down on his horn, the sound echoing in my ears. I watch the truck disappear in the mirror, my fear growing with each passing moment.

I'm shaking as I reach over to turn off the radio. As the truck falls into silence, Ben finally looks at me, anger in his eyes.

"Why did you turn off the music?" He reaches for the radio, and I bat his hand away. His fingers find the volume knob again, pushing my hand away in annoyance.

"Slow down, Ben! I'm scared! You're acting crazy. Please, Ben, please. Please, slow down." I'm crying now, snot making me blubbery. I can feel my entire body quaking; I see realization come into Ben's eyes. He looks at me, and I feel him take his foot off the pedal.

"Cleo, I'm sorr—" That's as far as he gets. A scream remains lodged in my throat as blood spatters across the windshield. He hits the brakes hard, tires squealing, as we slide across the road, and Ben fights to keep control of the truck. When we stop, I force my eyelids open and look into the glossy, dead eyes of a deer. I faint.

When I open them, Ben is leaning over me. While I've been out, he's successfully removed the deer from the windshield and all that remains is a gaping hole, splintered glass covering me and the dash. My face is wet, and when I rub it, I wipe away blood instead of tears. I'm not sure if the blood belongs to me, Ben, or the deer. With a shudder, I open the door and step out.

As soon as my feet hit pavement, I'm running toward the grass, falling to my knees. After I deposit the last of dinner on the ground, I stay seated there in disbelief. I feel him squat next to me, rubbing his hand down my back in comfort.

Instinctively, I jerk away from his touch, and he drops his hand.

"Why, Ben? Why did you do that?" My voice is a quiet whisper in the dark.

"I—" He starts, but I interrupt him.

"You know what happened to my parents, my whole family! My sister, Ben! My little sister!" I end with a hiss, and he flinches next to me. I stand up on shaky legs.

"Cleo, please, I'm sorry." He sounds sincere, but I can't care about that right now. He was reckless with not only his life but mine.

I shake my head. "No, Ben. It's not okay. I'm not okay. I... I think you should go. I can't be around you right now."

"What? Go? How will you get home? Let me take you home, Cleo." He's begging now, but I won't hear it. Not tonight.

"It's only a couple of miles. I'll walk." I turn from him then, walking quickly, head down, toward home. He stands still for a minute, watching me leave. Then I hear it—the sounds of the ignition turning over as he starts the truck and drives the opposite way.

If I had known then what I know now, I might have gone with him. Or maybe life would have turned out the same no matter what. The day after the accident, Ben left town and never looked back. I look at him now, tears of regret in his eyes, and my heart softens.

"I forgave you a long time ago, you know."

"Was that before or after you married my brother?" He says this softly, no hint of malice, only curiosity, in his tone.

"I'm sorry you were hurt. I was hurt, too. We've both made regrettable decisions, but I don't regret your brother. He loved me when I needed to be loved. And before you ask, yes, I loved him. How could I not?"

My heart squeezes as I think about Vincent. I didn't lie to Ben. The love I have for Vincent wasn't passionate, but it was a deeper kind of love I had shared with Ben. Vincent came to my rescue when he offered me his name. I'll always love him for that.

We stand in silence for several moments, remembering the past we share. Finally, Ben blows out a breath.

"Okay." He says it simply, as if there is no need for further discussion on the topic, and I feel the tension in my chest release.

"Okay," I say and mean it.

22

After a few more minutes of awkward chitchat, Ben steers the conversation back to the reason for his visit: the brown truck Macy saw here. An abandoned truck was located one town over that is registered to a man in Shaconage. That man? Mark Jeffers. Like a sucker punch to the gut, it winds me, and I find my way to the table and take a seat there.

"Are you serious?" I ask.

"It's not a sure sign of guilt, you understand, but it is suspicious that Mark was seen at Dahlia's house so close to the attack."

"Have you talked to him? Did he give any explanation?" My mind is racing, all the possibilities swirling with one question glaring at me: Was this an act of revenge?

"We haven't been able to make contact yet. When we find him, I'll tell you immediately. But that brings me to the next thing. You need to find somewhere to stay."

"I can take care of myself, Ben."

"Humor me, please. I'd suggest you stay with Macy, but if that's an issue..." He leaves the rest unsaid, and I swallow hard. I can't stay with him, not with emotions as tangled as they are.

"No, it's fine. I'll call Macy. I'm sure she'll let me stay with her." Especially if staying with Ben is my only other option. "You'll let me know when I can come back home?"

"I promise."

I nod and stand up. "Okay. I'll call Macy, and then I'll be ready to go." I walk to the back of the house and enter my room, closing the door quietly behind me with a click.

To her credit, Macy doesn't ask questions and lets me settle into her guest room without complaint. The room is decorated in soft pinks and greens with French doors that open to the garden, which is planted with a riot of roses in every color imaginable.

I take time to wash my face and change into pajamas before calling Netta. After explaining I'd be staying with Macy, I hang up and pad to the kitchen, where I find her opening takeout containers of chicken parmesan.

"Hey," I say quietly, still unsure of where we stand.

She smiles at me and offers a piece of garlic bread. I take a bite and groan dramatically.

Laughing, she gives my shoulder a push.

"If you'll open some wine, I'll get this on the table."

My stomach grumbles at the thought of a proper dinner, and I happily oblige.

After dinner, we take our wine to the front porch. One of the things I've missed the most about home is sitting on the porch after dinner, listening to the cicadas. We sit in silence for a while, rocking back and forth on the porch swing.

I tell Macy about Trevor and the trip to Atlanta. Talking about it doesn't make it more bearable, necessarily, but it does give me a sense of control over my story. That doesn't mean I'm going to run out in the streets and tell everyone or take out an ad in the paper, but it's no longer this shameful secret. Instead, I've pulled it into the light. It can't hurt me anymore.

When I finish, I let out a sigh of relief. No more secrets. My heart feels lighter than it has since I was a kid. She took my hand while I spoke, and I give it a gentle squeeze now, grateful to have her support and friendship. She squeezes back, and when I look at her, I'm surprised to see tears in her eyes.

"Macy, it's okay. I'm okay. I promise." Instead of replying, she shakes her head three times quickly, and fat drops pour from her eyes. She closes them and lets out a small whimper.

I'm at a loss. I'm touched, but I'm also feeling uneasy. It's not my intention to make her feel bad for something she had no part of. Ever the nurturer, I pull her into a hug, and she quiets. Finally, she speaks.

"It's just...I'm sorry. I pushed you away back then, and I've pushed you away now. And for what? If I hadn't been so angry about Ben and gone back to the hotel early, you wouldn't have been alone with Trevor in that car. And if I hadn't done the exact same thing this week, you would have had me with you in Atlanta. I'm so sorry, Cleo." She says the last in a small voice, and I rub her back in small circles, trying to comfort her in her unnecessary guilt. It was never her job to keep me safe. It was Trevor's job to be a good man—or even a halfway decent one. He failed.

I'm ready to respond and reassure her when I hear someone clear their throat. At the sound, Macy and I both jump. I stand, whirling toward the edge of the porch, where I can see a figure standing just beyond the porch light's reach.

"Who's there?" Even to my ears, I can tell my voice is strained. Willing myself to calm down, I take a steadying breath.

With a chuckle, a man steps out of the shadows and into the glow of the porch light. Devin Mathews. Beside me, Macy bristles and stands, but I wave her off. I guess today's the day to face demons.

"Mr. Mathews. What brings you here?" I'm proud of the steel I hear in my question. My tone says, "fuck off, dickhead" and I almost smile, but I force myself to remain still, arms crossed as we face off.

Despite my tone and body language, Devin remains unfazed, walking toward me slowly with a lazy gait. If anything, he seems more curious than ever—the opposite of what I'd like to see.

"Miss Cleo. I heard you were back in town. Pity about your grandmother. Dahlia was always a bit of a hard ass.

Lord knows she never shared a drop of information about you."

I take a quick step forward, ready to wring his scrawny neck when Macy stops me with a hand on the shoulder. At that, his face transforms into a leer as he delivers the final blow.

"Then again," he says, "maybe she knew as little about you as the rest of us. It's not like you visit. I'm surprised you've returned at all, but I guess someone has to plan the funeral."

"YOU ASSHOLE!" It explodes from me, and I feel fury slither up my legs like flames. I'm going to break his fucking face. Macy has me gripped tight, but I shake her off and lunge toward him; my long legs have me before his shorter frame within seconds. I don't have time to consider it before my fist is breaking his nose in a satisfying crack. The force of it has him stumbling backward, his hand going to his face. I can't help the smirk that blossoms when I see droplets of blood.

He glares at me through his red-stained fingers, a handkerchief materializing from his pocket to staunch the flow. He coughs a couple of times and spits pink-tinted phlegm on the grass.

"You should leave." Macy has stepped between us to prevent further bloodshed, I'm sure. Even though I'm the taller of the two of us, she carries herself with more confidence, and I can see Devin hesitate before finally stepping back with a nod.

"I only came here to request Cleo give a formal interview for an upcoming anniversary piece."

"Anniversary piece?"

"Surely even you remember your wedding anniversary, Cleo." His voice, muffled behind the cloth, drips with condescension.

"Get out of here, Devin, or so help me God, I'll give you a black eye to match."

"I'll quote you as no comment, then?" I lunge at him, ready to make good on my threat. He laughs as he jumps back. He turns to leave before stopping to look back at me. "You think about it and call me at this number." He offers me a card and sets it on the railing when I don't take it. "I'd like to give you an opportunity to clear some things up before I publish. I know things about you, Cleo. Things you might not want out." He holds my gaze for several long seconds before he turns and leaves for good. When he's gone, I sag against the banister. My mind swirls with trepidation, sweat breaks out across my brow. What does he know?

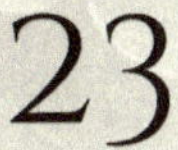

23

She really is beautiful. Not in the traditional sense. Cleo is too tall for that. No, Cleo is beautiful in the way she talks, the way she walks, and even in the way she sleeps.

Through the French doors, Love watches Cleo sleep. It would be so easy to slip into the room with her, to finally make everything known—the sacrifices, the plans. Love has waited a while, too long, to mess this up.

Soon, Cleo will accept Love as her everything.

The rest of the night passed without incident, yet unsurprisingly, sleep eluded me. Macy had errands this morning, so I'm on my own for a while. I'm eating a bowl of cereal when I get a text message from Ben.

Call me

Without much thought, I pull up his contact and hit the call button. I'm considering a second bowl of Cocoa Puffs when he answers.

"DeMarco." His gruff greeting and tone throw me off.

I squeak out, "Hey," and wait for him to speak again.

"Oh, Cleo. I thought you were someone else. Good news. We caught up with Jeffers. Unfortunately, we didn't learn much from him. He claims the truck was stolen back in February. He says he filed a police report over in Maryville. I'm waiting for confirmation now. Looks like we'll be cutting him loose later."

"You're letting him go?" What does this mean for Dahlia's case? Macy saw the truck. It must be connected.

"We don't have a choice. We can't hold him without more than the truck to go on. I'm sorry."

"Will you at least check it for fingerprints? That's a thing, right?"

"Cleo, leave the investigation to me. I have this under control." I chew on my nail as I consider my options.

"Fine, but I'm going home. I can't put everything on hold over this. I need to sleep in my own bed, and I really should spend more time at the hospital with Dahlia."

"We'll talk about it."

I don't like his tone. "There's no 'we' in this decision. It's mine alone, Ben. I'm going home. Let me know when you find out if he made a report." I hang up and throw the phone at the couch before going to the guest room to retrieve my bag.

I see them the moment I step into the house. Sticky notes. Hundreds of them cover the walls and furniture of the front room. From my position by the door, I can see they continue, covering the walls that disappear down the hall toward my bedroom.

Curious despite my trepidation, I take two steps forward to read a solitary note attached to the ancient rotary phone in the foyer. "I <3 U" is scrawled across its yellow surface, the handwriting reminiscent of a third grader's cursive penmanship.

"Hello?" I say, my voice shattering the silence yet somehow only adding to my growing unease. I don't know why I call out. Do I really want someone to respond? Quickly, I back toward the door, not stopping until I feel the knob digging into my lower back. The door rattles as I make contact, urging me to leave. I pull my cell from my back pocket and dial Ben's number, eyes darting between the phone and the empty rooms beyond my immediate line of vision.

Ben arrives quickly, tires squealing as he careens into the driveway. I left the front room after calling him, unable to stand the quiet any longer. I don't move from my spot when I hear him arrive. He finds me in the backyard on the tire swing.

I quickly realized that whoever left those notes was long gone. Once I could rationalize that to myself, I felt calmer and comfortable enough to wait around for Ben. It's no big deal to wait outside, far from the weirdness inside the house. But there is one thing for sure—I'm not going back in until he goes with me.

We move from room to room, scanning for any missing objects as we go, but nothing is out of place. The only items that don't belong are the hundreds of sticky notes meticulously placed throughout the house. And, if I knew and welcomed sweet gestures, a sticky note here and there wouldn't be unnerving. But this wasn't a simple sticky note from a lover. There were sticky notes on every free surface and in places they really shouldn't be.

What I found most unsettling was a sticky note I found in the kitchen. On the knife block, of all places. What kind of message is that supposed to send? Nothing says I love you like a reminder that an unknown stranger has been in your house, especially when that reminder is attached to a sharp object. I mean, *Jesus*. Who is this sick fuck?

When we finally open the door to my bedroom, I am completely unfazed. Numb. Across the bed are hundreds of flower petals. Upon closer inspection, it's clear that they are dahlias. I feel Ben's eyes on me as I circle the bed, studying the flowers. Multiple varieties are repre-sented: Dahlia imperialis, pinnata, cactus, and mignon to name a few. I stop short when I see my favorites nestled in the center. The pompon was my signature flower growing up.

"I don't understand it, Ben. None of this makes sense." My shoulders ache, but I make myself stand tall. If my stalker is watching me, which I suspect he always is, I will not give him the satisfaction of seeing me fall apart. I can't continue to be his victim. But as strong as I know I need to be, I know that I can't stay here any longer. Sleeping in this house is no longer safe for me.

"Is your couch still free?" I say it casually, hoping he can't see how nervous he can still make me. I give Ben a small smile and jerk a thumb toward my still-packed suitcase. With a grunt, he picks it up and motions me toward the door with a flick of his head.

"Let's go."

I don't take anything else from the house when we leave. I lock the front door and wait while Ben walks the perimeter before joining me.

"What should we do about the notes?" I can feel another round of acid reflux beginning to inch its way up my throat and consider returning to the house to grab a bottle of TUMS. On second thought, I'll just buy another at the drugstore. Nothing could make me go back in there right now. Nothing. Thankfully, Ben doesn't ask me to.

"I'll have Deputy Franks and a crew come by and take care of it. To preserve any DNA evidence, it should be handled by professionals, anyway." He pauses for a moment, head tilted as he studies the house.

"What?" It's not like Ben to hold back, especially with me.

"What kind of flowers were those on the bed?"

"You didn't recognize them?" It's not surprising. When we dated, I think he gave me flowers once, and that was a grocery store bouquet the day of prom. I'm sure he grabbed the closest bunch near the register and didn't even look at them.

"Should I? Clearly, they weren't roses. I do know those. I might not know much about flowers, but you seemed to grow more upset once you got a good look at them. "

I hold his gaze for a moment before replying. "They were dahlias."

"What the fuck?" he whispers, throwing a glance over his shoulder at the house.

"Yeah. They're also my favorite flower. Do you know what the Dahlia represents in the language of flowers?"

"I didn't even know there was a flower language. You're serious?"

"I'm completely serious. Go ahead. Ask me."

"What's a Dahlia mean?"

I never break eye contact, so I flinch when I see the fury that comes into his eyes at my answer. "Everlasting love." Tears come to my eyes as I say it, the horror of it hitting me all at once.

Whomever this person is, this stalker, they don't intend to ever let me go. This will never end.

25

I can't help but laugh when we arrive at the police station, and Ben takes my bag from the back of the Jeep.

"You live at the station?" My laugh is a giggle, and I shake my head at the absurdity of it all. It seems I run the full gamut of emotions every time I'm with Ben.

He shakes his head, disbelief in his eyes. "Do you think the job is my whole life? Lord, Cleo. I do have more going on besides small-town police work."

"Sorry, Ben. Of course, you have a life." My tone is mocking, and I make sure to put just enough disbelief in my tone to make it seem I doubt the possibility. He doesn't take offense. If anything, the banter puts him at ease.

His grin grows large, perfect teeth gleaming. "I thought maybe you'd be more comfortable in a cell where we can keep a close watch on you." My smile drops at that, and I come to a full stop in the middle of the street. "Wait, what?" I look between Ben and the station, mouth open wide like a guppy.

"Oh, my god. You should see your face right now. I'm kidding, Cleo. My apartment sits above the station." I shove his shoulder hard, and he jumps away from me with a smile. Pulling a set of keys from his pocket, he opens a blue door next to the entrance to the police station. Self-conscious, I let my gaze drift around the parking lot and nearby businesses, anxious to get upstairs before the entire town sees me at Ben's place. Of course, he'd have a place in town.

He pulls the door wide, and I dart inside, allowing him to shut it behind me. He takes the stairs two at a time with my suitcase, but I follow at a much slower pace, nerves combining with a touch of excitement at the prospect of spending more time with him.

I'll need to call Netta and tell her to steer clear of Dahlia's house. I'm sure Ben can go out with me to take care of the chickens sometime tomorrow. The last thing I want is for Netta to be threatened or harmed. It's best to keep her out of this mess as much as possible. After that, I'll need to fill in Macy on the latest message from my stalker. There's a possibility she might be upset I chose to come to Ben's instead of her house. But, again, this isn't her fight; it's mine. The further she is from the perpetrator's radar, the better.

Ben is the best option. As much as it pains me to admit it, he's my only chance of finding Dahlia's attacker, the one person capable of keeping me safe. Isn't there a saying about that? The enemy of my enemy is my friend. And while it's true that Ben and I have a long way to go in mending our own relationship, he's the best I have and—more than that—he's not half bad. He's grown in the years we've been apart. He's mature and confident in a way he could never quite pull off when we were kids. Sure, he strutted around this town like a king, but deep down, he was just as scared as the rest of us. And when push came to shove, when it came down to holding his ground or fleeing, he left in the night.

I shake my head in an attempt to clear the cobwebs of yesterday's regrets and quicken my pace, coming to stand behind Ben at the top of the stairs. The apartment is larger than I expected a space above a business to be. Removing my satchel, I place it on top of the wall beside the stairs and move farther into the apartment. I'm not sure apartment is the right word exactly. From what little I can see from here, Ben's place is more comparable to a small house or large condo than an apartment.

Floor-to-ceiling windows, completely bare of blinds or curtains, make up the back wall of the living room. At the top, tastefully hidden, is a row of shades. Aesthetically, the open, bare windows make the space feel more inviting than cold and sterile. Behind the window wall sits the forest and the backyard of the police station. A small, fenced rec yard is the only structure abutting the thick copse of greenery.

Moving away from the windows, I notice the kitchen, and Ben follows me silently into it, watching as I peruse his cabinets. The kitchen is gorgeous, but it seems unused. A pity since he has beautiful cookware. Were these a gift from Mariah, or worse, a girlfriend?

It occurs to me that I haven't even asked Ben about

his life. It shames me to admit I never gave it a thought. And I don't mean asking about his hobbies or what books he read this year. It's possible Ben has a girlfriend, maybe even a fiancée. Though I'm sure if he had one, Mariah would have made that clear to me when she accosted me at Dahlia's.

"It was presumptuous of me to ask to stay here. Is this okay? I don't want to cause any issues for you with your mom...or a girlfriend." The question is in my statement. Ben can share what he wants, and if he doesn't, that's his prerogative, too.

"Thanks for your concern, but I can handle my mom. As far as girlfriends go, I'm currently single. Zara moved to Connecticut for a job with ESPN last year, and we both thought it best to end things on a friendly note." I make a non-committal sound, content to let him interpret that how he'd like. There's not much else I can do but trust him to handle any issues that might crop up with his parents. I opt to forego any conversation about his ex. Ben isn't mine, and he isn't hers, so why should I let tiny tendrils of jealousy take hold? No, it's best to let that one alone.

French doors open onto the balcony where I can see wicker furniture and a grill. I'm sure Mariah is responsible for the furniture. I can't see Ben picking out white wicker and floral patterns on his own.

The rest of our tour reveals two bedrooms and two full baths as well as a small office. Ben's apartment is larger than Dahlia's entire house. The bedrooms are on opposite sides of the space, and after he shows me in, he leaves me to settle into the guest room. Unsure of how long I'll be here, I unpack my suitcase and find space for everything, including a spot by the window for my easel. A quick glance outside alerts me to a tree that houses a family of squirrels that my fingers are aching to paint.

I pull out my cell and send a text to Macy, letting her know there was an incident and that I'd be staying at Ben's place. She doesn't immediately respond, so I move on to Netta. The phone rings several times before she answers. I can't help but expel a sigh of relief when she does.

"Hey, Netta." I smile at the joy I hear in her voice at my call. No matter what happens here with Dahlia, I know I can't neglect Netta any further. She's always given her love and support so unconditionally to me. She deserves better.

"Hey, sweet pea! I just left Dahlia. I'm glad I spent the last couple of days there because I was able to see the doctor this morning when she came by for her rounds. The doc says she's showing good signs. She might wake up! The doctor said she'll be calling you in a bit to fill you in."

At that, my heart leaps. Dahlia might wake up. I can't help the tears that come to my eyes, and I'm unsurprised when Ben comes to the door, questions in his eyes at the sound of my sobs.

"What is it?" He mouths the words to me, and I shake my head, a tremulous smile forming. I hold up one finger to wait, and he nods, leaning against the frame.

"Netta, that's great news! I'll call the doctor myself when we hang up. I was calling to ask you a favor. There's been some drama over at Dahlia's house the last couple of days, and I really need you to stay away from there for a bit. Can you do that? Ben is going to take care of the chickens, so don't worry about them. Okay?"

"If there's trouble at Dee's place, where are you gonna be?"

"I'm staying at Ben's place for now."

I hear the relief in her voice when she replies, "Yes, Cleo. Stay with Ben. He can take care of you. Dahlia would want you to stay with him." Satisfied I'm well cared for, Netta lays out chicken care instructions, and I pretend to be writing them down while she speaks, occasionally repeating a word or two back to her. When she's done, she reminds me to call the doctor. We hang up with a promise to meet at the hospital tomorrow morning.

Quickly, I fill Ben in on Dahlia's prognosis. He recovers from his own shock quickly and leaves the room to call the hospital himself. Hopeful and jubilant, I send Macy a text with the news, asking if she'd like to come with us tomorrow. After speaking with the doctor, Ben calls his friends in Maryville and requests an officer be placed outside Dahlia's hospital room. This could all be over soon.

26

Things seem to fall into place after the call with Netta. Within half an hour, Ben goes downstairs to the station to question Mark Jeffers, who was located at a bar in Rockwood late last night. He had a bit too much to drink and was brought in to sleep it off. Once he was booked, it was found he was wanted for questioning here. Ben arranged a quick transport, once again calling in favors. He's lucky his dad is such a well-known attorney. Money speaks, I guess.

I was uninterested in observing the interview downstairs. Either he has something to do with the case, or he doesn't. It's Ben's job to find out. Instead, I call the doctor assigned to Dahlia's care.

Within the last day, Dahlia has begun to respond to painful stimuli. Just this morning, she moved her fingers when asked. If Dahlia wakes up, there's no guarantee she will remember anything about her accident. And if she wakes up, we should let her rest and take it slowly. In other words, we shouldn't expect to interrogate her. We are, however, encouraged to visit and talk with Dahlia, in hopes it will help her wake up.

After the call, I take a shower, reveling in the brand-new shower in the guest bath. The water pressure here puts Dahlia's to shame. The scalding jets beat my aching shoulders, and I stay under them as long as possible, drawing out the feeling.

I'm in the bedroom, toweling off, when I hear Ben come back into the house. The sounds of him rummaging through the cabinets makes me smile. I forgot how comforting it is to have another person around. I've been on my own for far too long.

I'm dressed in running shorts, and I'm pulling a faded T-shirt over my head when Ben barrels into the room. He stops short at my gasp. With jerking movements, I yank the edges of the shirt, covering my abdomen from view. Too late, I realize immediately. Ben's eyes are glued to the space now covered by the T-shirt, the gnarled edges of a scar I know by heart.

"Is that from the accident?" he asks, his eyes still on the T-shirt.

With a swallow, I clear my throat but don't speak. Instead, I simply nod. I don't make eye contact. It's too raw. Not only did he see me without my shirt, but he saw the scar—the ugly part of me that I'll carry forever. It's a reminder of all my losses. Losses I can't fully explain to Ben right now, perhaps ever.

I almost don't hear him when he asks, his words are so soft. The gentle caress of his voice rips me in two. "Can I see it?"

It's hard to articulate why, but I need him to see it. I

want to say I'm a real person. I bleed. I hurt. I want him to see what loving him—and Vincent and the baby—had given me. More than emotional scars, I have permanent, physical ones. I make eye contact now, holding his gaze in a steady, unflinching moment of honesty.

"Yes." My response is simple but effective. He walks toward me slowly, as if worried he might spook me, his hands at his sides while his gaze holds mine. Suddenly calm, it's easy to lift the corner of my shirt and let him see all of me.

I pull off my shirt, upper body bare but for a sports bra. I watch as his eyes trace the scar that snakes from my belly button and across my right side before disappearing to slither around to my back, finally stopping just short of my spine. Even after all these years, it's raised, and while no longer red, it remains a contrasting darkened pink against my pale complexion. I'm fine with it. It's a forever reminder of what I've lost, a battle scar that shows I'm a survivor.

He hesitates before reaching out to touch its edges with his fingers, their calloused tips both soft and rough. I close my eyes, allowing his touch to soothe a long-ago hurt. Slowly, achingly slow, he follows each branch and whorl of the scar with expert care and gentleness. At first, he traces it in its entirety. Then he takes his time, rubbing each individual piece of the scar, over and over again, like he's willing it to disappear under his touch.

I don't know how long he touches me, but it's over too soon. As he steps back from me, I feel an ache settle within my heart. *Watch it, Cleo.* I tell myself firmly. *He's not for you.* When he finally pulls me into a hug, I hug him back, despite the warning bells going off in my head. He simply holds me there, his arms tight and warm around me. And through it all, he repeats a mantra I no longer need but appreciate.

"I'm sorry, Cleo. I'm so sorry." He doesn't elaborate, and I don't need him to. Instead, I tell him the same. And when it's all over, I no longer see the boy who left me behind, but a man who will do anything to make sure I'm never hurt again. I believe him. This time, I know he won't let me down.

27

The moment is interrupted when my phone rings. Bennett lets go of me, and I step back, giving him a shy glance as I go. I feel flushed and slightly giddy, so it's no surprise to me that I'm slightly breathless when I answer.

"This is Cleo." I glance at Ben out of the corner of my eye. He is staring at his own phone, leaning against the long dresser in front of the bed.

"Cleo, it's Tate. You sound winded. Is this a bad time?" My smile drops and guilt hits me. I'm not sure why, but a feeling of unfaithfulness rolls through me. But we're not together, not really...right? I bite my lip and turn from Ben to face the adjoining bath.

"Uh, hey, Tate. No, it's not a bad time. I was hoping you'd call today." My voice softens as I tell him about Dahlia.

"Sweetheart, that's wonderful. I know how much this means to you. Hopefully, she'll be able to give some answers soon."

Sweetheart? My heart swells at the endearment, yet I catch myself looking over at Ben to see if he heard. He continues to stare at his phone, oblivious to the conversation.

"Yeah, we, uh, hope to know more soon. I wanted to tell you I made the report in Atlanta. About Trevor. It's done." From the corner of my eye, I can see Ben has straightened from his slouched position at the mention of Trevor. I ignore him and focus on what Tate's saying instead.

"I'm glad. Listen, about that...you should really talk to the sheriff about Trevor's visits to your grandmother. I'm not saying they're related, but you've mentioned the harassment you dealt with from him when you were young, and I wonder if he could be responsible. His cell pinged near Dahlia's house just hours before her accident."

"Yes, but his parents live just down the street. Logically, he may have just been visiting them there."

"Just talk to him about it, okay?"

"Of course. I'm sure the sheriff will look into it. Anything else?" As much as I love talking to Tate, I'm too aware of Ben's presence in the room, especially after he just had his hands on me, to focus on anything Tate's saying. Not to mention the fact that I'm riddled with guilt. If Tate wants to be official, then maybe I should feel guilty. But as of yet, we haven't even said we're dating. Relax, Cleo. Relax.

"Actually, there is more." I hear paper rustling as he puts me on speakerphone. "You asked me to find out more about Devin Mathews, and I put my best guy on it.

Turns out, he's been in Phoenix as recently as three weeks ago. According to my investigator, he's been visiting your galleries and asking questions. I don't know how he did it, but he's been at The Hope Center too. How he even got that address is a mystery to me. Believe me, I'll figure it out. I don't like the idea of our girls being vulnerable. The implications don't sit well with me. You need to be careful around him."

I knew Devin was obsessed with the accident, and I'm aware he's made money off of my pain, but what can he have to gain off a story over a decade old? It doesn't make sense. Tate continues to list Devin's whereabouts and financials, but my mind is elsewhere. I can't help but think of his last words to me. Maybe it's time to talk to Devin myself.

"I'm not asking you to come home, Cleo. You know I want you here more than anything, especially after that last night together, but I won't ask you to leave Dahlia. I know how much she means to you."

"Thank you, Tate. I'll call you tomorrow and let you know what the doctor said, okay?"

"Sounds good. I miss you."

"Miss you too." I hang up without another word, feeling gutted. Shaconage has a way of making the rest of the world seem insignificant. Not ten minutes ago, I had my shirt off, and Ben was touching my skin like a lover. Something I never should have let happen. Overwhelmed by conflicting feelings, I rub small circles on my forehead before turning back to Ben, who is no longer staring at his phone. Ben, who suddenly seems very interested in my conversation.

"Who is Tate?" he says, each word clipped and controlled.

I take a tentative step forward as I speak. "Tate is a friend—well, he's a friend, but he's also my attorney and advisor. We've been together a long time." I say it nonchalantly but realize too late how the last sentence sounded. Ben calmly sets his phone on the dresser and stands up to his full height.

"I—" I begin, but he doesn't let me finish. Before I can process that he's moved, his mouth is on mine. One, two, three steps and my back slams against the wall by the door. The sculpted ridges of his abdomen press into me as his body holds me captive against the wall. His hand finds the bottom of my top, sliding up my stomach to grab my breast. Want rolls through me like a sigh when his fingertips brush my nipple. At his squeeze, I feel that same desire zip through me, and I am surprised when I moan long and deep into his mouth.

He releases my breast and pulls his hand out of my shirt to cup my face in his hands. I feel his tongue pressing against my lips insistently, and I open my mouth, letting him in. Impossibly, he pulls me closer as he presses his tongue deeper still, pulling me into a maelstrom of emotions. It's both too wonderful and too much.

With absolutely no force behind it, I push at his chest. It's enough, and he breaks the contact, his gaze hooded as he looks down at me, his blue eyes almost black with emotion. Outwardly, he appears calm—the exact opposite of my own emotions. I'm being tossed about in a tornado of emotion, yet he seems unfazed, untouched. He remains impossibly close to me, and I can feel his breath against my cheek. I shiver, my body aching to continue where we left off. I close my eyes and take a deep breath. I need to gain control of this conversation.

"Tate—"

"Don't say his name to me right now, or so help me God, Cleo, you're going to find yourself flat on your back in that bed." His words are low and dangerous, and I jerk when I feel his hand on my arm, molten like lava. My eyes follow his hand, up his arm, until I finally make eye contact again and realize my mistake. He isn't calm. He's the eye of the storm, and he wants to sweep me up and away. A part of me wants to see how far I can push him, to see what he might do. Another part of me is scared shitless. Fear wins, and I step to the side, breaking eye contact.

I pick my phone up from the floor where I dropped it when he kissed me and sit it on the bed without looking at the screen. I clear my throat.

"Were you going to tell me Trevor comes to town, or were you going to keep that to yourself?"

He sighs and walks to the window, his gaze unreadable.

"He hasn't been here since you've come back. I didn't want to add to your worry."

"Don't you think he warrants looking into? I mean, he was here the day Dahlia was attacked, and I've told you what he's capable of."

"I agree it's a huge coincidence. I do. It's possible he's the attacker, but he's not your stalker."

"How can you be so sure?" He walks over to the dresser and picks up his phone, scrolling until he finds Instagram, and opens it before handing it over to me. My gut clenches at the sight of Trevor's face, but I ignore it as I watch the Insta Story from yesterday and today. Trevor is in the Bahamas. He's been there all week and, based on the tags on his page, there are dozens of photos and videos to prove it.

I hand the phone back to Ben and walk out into the living room. I take a seat in the middle of the couch and curl up with an oversized pillow. Ben silently follows me into the room and sits opposite me in a high-back chair.

"What now?" I ask, the weariness seeping out of my voice, saturating the quiet room in its hopelessness.

"I'll talk to Devin next, since I'll need his alibi now, too. I came up here to tell you about my interview with Jeffers, but I got distracted." My cheeks warm at that, and I laugh, desperate to dispel the awkwardness I feel.

"Okay, so how did it go?"

"Well, Jeffers didn't give me much. Said he wasn't ever at Dahlia's house and doesn't even know where she lives. I find that hard to believe, honestly, since everyone knows that house. It's one of the oldest in town."

I nod at that. Dahlia's grandpa built it himself shortly after setting up camp here.

"So, anyway, he said he wasn't saying anything else without a lawyer and demanded to leave if he wasn't being charged. He left an hour ago." He shrugs as if to say, that's how it goes. We sit in silence for a while.

We're no closer to knowing who hurt Dahlia than we were yesterday, yet it feels like we're getting close. I can't help but think I already know who it is, but I'm missing something important.

Mentally, I review what I know. First, Dahlia was attacked by someone who wanted to force me to come home. This person knows me or knew of me before I left. Of course, that doesn't narrow it down much, considering how small Shaconage is. This brings me to the next item. Dahlia received notes, steadily, until she was attacked. Those notes have no fingerprints on them, which means whoever is doing this is smart and meticulous. Third, my stalker has knowledge of me on an intimate level. My favorite flower was left on the bed.

"Oh, my god." I sit up suddenly, groping for my phone in the cushions.

"What is it?" Ben has come to sit beside me on the couch, alert and concerned.

I ignore him for a moment, pulling up google and typing in "Camellia flower meaning" before pressing the search icon. With a satisfied grin, I hand the phone to Ben so he can read it.

Camellia: love, adoration, longing.

With a grim look, he hands the phone back to me and pulls out his own phone. He keys in a number and puts the phone to his ear, holding my gaze as we wait for an answer.

"Alice, it's Ben DeMarco. I was wondering if I could come down to talk to you about some flowers. Maybe ten minutes?"

Soon, we're out the door and on our way to Pocketful of Posies on Main Street. We walk there quickly, our feet eating up the pavement as we go.

I'm out of breath when we arrive, eager to see what Alice might know. At our entrance, she whirls from the cutting counter, shears pressed to her heart.

"Oh my god, y'all gave me a fright."

I do my best not to roll my eyes. We told her we were on our way less than five minutes ago.

"Alice, put down the shears. You're gonna hurt yourself." I point to the tip as I speak. An inch higher and she'll cut her neck.

"Oh, gosh. That's funny." She lets out a braying laugh and waves the shears in the air between us. Her moods ever-changing, Alice goes serious, laying aside the shears to take my hand in hers. "How is your granny? We've been worried sick about her down at the church. Ain't nobody knows how to plan the Labor Day picnic like her."

"There's not much to say right now, but when we know more, we'll be sure to let everyone at the church know. I'm sure she'd be touched to know everyone is thinking of her." If only Dahlia were able to enjoy this part. She'd get a kick out of the fake sympathies and concern of her fellow church members. She'd agree with my assessment that Alice's concern was only a front to see what gossip she might glean. Alice is the gossip queen in Shaconage...which can come in handy, I suppose, when your family isn't the source of it.

"Anyway, Alice, we need to ask you about recent flower orders." This from Ben, who has no patience for small talk or pleasantries. Which is fine by me. "Have you had any orders for dahlias or camellias lately?"

"Is this official police business?" Her eyes narrow as

she glances between the two of us, assessing. Okay. Best to handle this as delicately as possible.

"It's for me, actually. It looks like someone left some flowers for Dahlia at the hospital, and we're just trying to figure out who left them. So we can thank them." She seems to take my word for it, shrugs, and turns to her desktop.

"Huh. It doesn't look like we've had any recent orders for those here. To be honest, we don't get a lot of orders for dahlias. Camellias, sure. Those are what I like to call 'filler flowers.' Since your granny is at the hospital over in Maryville, you might want to check some florists there."

We thank her and leave before she can ask more probing questions, such as why Ben and I are at the shop together. We walk back to his apartment, and I throw a quick look over my shoulder, just in time to see Alice's face peer at us from the window. I swear I see her take a photo. That's just great. By dinner, everyone in town will know I'm staying at Ben's.

Sometimes I hate being right. Within an hour, I get a text from Macy with a screenshot attached. Some of the girls from high school sent her texts, asking if Ben and I were "back together." While texting with Macy, who did not give me grief about staying with Ben instead of with her, I hear Ben on the phone with his mother in the other room.

Heated words in low tones drift through the apartment, though I can't make out any of the conversation. He answered the phone, but once the conversation began, he swiftly walked outside to the balcony to speak to her with his back to me. It's for the best I don't hear it, anyway.

I'm doing my best to ignore them when I hear a crash and the sound of an alarm blaring from outside. I rush to the window facing the street, only to see several people gathered around my Jeep. The sound of the alarm draws Ben inside and he ends his call when he sees me run down the stairs. He follows, steps quick on the stairs behind me. I ignore the stares as we exit the apartment.

"Excuse me, please," I tell several people hovering over the Jeep. I fumble for my keys, pulling them out of the satchel as I reach the side door. I drop the keys when I see the cause of the commotion. A brick has been thrown through the window, and I can see a sheet of paper held around it by a rubber band. I barely give it notice. Instead, my eyes focus on one word scrawled in an angry red across the driver's door.

"TRAMP" glares at me. Beside me, Ben curses. He picks up the keys and silences the alarm, telling the gawkers to go home. I'm afraid to look at my neighbors, afraid to see if they agree that I'm a tramp. Ben pulls a pair of gloves from his pocket before reaching into the back seat to retrieve the brick. He unfolds the letter and reads it, his eyes growing darker with each passing moment. I step forward to take the note from him.

To my unfaithful bride—

Imagine my surprise to learn you'd gone crawling back to Bennett DeMarco. Haven't I already given you a second chance? Must I make it three? You know what they say, Fool me once...

I don't want to keep on punishing you, but you seem to continuously choose the hard way. You didn't learn with Vincent, and it seems, you haven't learned after Dahlia. This is your last warning, Cleo.

My patience is wearing thin.

I hear Ben calling for Deputy Franks as he makes his way back to the station. I don't follow him. Instead, I stay near the car and continue to stare at the ground, my mind drifting away as it sometimes does when things get too difficult. I'm startled when I feel a soft hand on my arm. I jerk from the touch, so unexpected. When I look up, I'm surprised to find I'm not alone.

There are several ladies standing next to me. Some I recognize as friends of Dahlia, but others are women I've grown up with. I see Alice standing among them, and my heart drops. Another piece of news for the gossip mill, I guess.

"I'm...sorry." I don't know what else to say. I'm hurt that someone would be so bold, so fearless, to vandalize my car in broad daylight. But more than that, I'm sorry that the whole town is seeing my private drama. I know I'm not a tramp, but they don't. All they see are the words written on the Jeep...and my exit from Ben's apartment. To them, I must certainly look like one. But it looks like there's more than one surprise in store for me today.

"You don't have one thing to be sorry for, Cleo Boucher." I make eye contact with Marlene from the bank. She has a fierce look on her face. One that dares everyone around me to say one nasty word. Unbidden, tears come to my eyes, though I try to stop them.

"That's right. I'm sick and tired of everyone in this town gossiping about you and Ben. You're grown-ups. You can do what you want. There is no call for anyone to write such a thing on your car." That was from Cathy at the post office.

Alice, whom I'm certain told everyone where I'm staying, nodded her head in agreement. Okay, I'll let her by with that one. She keeps looking at the car, eyes wide, and I'm sure I see tears forming in them even now.

I sigh and run my fingers along the car. I'm quiet, and no one speaks, but they stay standing with me, their faces in various stages of despair. It's funny, really. A decade ago, I craved their acceptance, and they refused to give it. Now they are throwing it at me. I trace the "T" for a moment, considering my options.

Ben won't be happy with my decision, but now that I've made up my mind, there's no changing it. I turn to find six pairs of expectant eyes on me. I give a watery smile at the group and clear my throat.

"I'm wondering if I can ask you guys some questions about Dahlia." The women around me wear identical puzzled expressions, clearly wondering what Dahlia could have to do with the spray paint on my car.

"Do you see this?" I point to the car and wave the note wildly. Again, they nod their matching looks of bafflement. "The same person who did this hurt Dahlia. And all to force me back to town. This whole thing is so I'd come back here. I've been wracking my brain for days, and I've come up with absolutely nothing, absolutely no one who would want to hurt her. And the more I look for them, the less I know. Dahlia might never wake up, and I need you guys to think hard about who she might have been seen with lately. I need your help. *Please.*"

"Cleo!" Ben has returned with his deputy, and from his tone, I can tell he is not on board. "That's enough. Stop getting involved and let me handle this, damn it." He's close to me now, and he grips my arm to move me away from the group of women.

I'm not prepared when Cathy wallops him on the arm. "Don't you get high and mighty, Ben DeMarco, and don't you bully the girl." She gives him two more smacks for good measure before turning back to me. "I won't lie, Cleo. Just like the rest, I assumed you came back to bury Dahlia and break Ben's heart again. Honestly, after you ran out on Vincent's funeral, none of us have been happy to see you back."

I hear Ben grunt beside me, but thankfully, he keeps his mouth shut.

I grimace but don't comment either. As I said, there is no lost love for me in Shaconage.

"But I can admit when I'm wrong. I won't comment on you coming out of Ben's place because I think that's a bad idea, and Mariah will be livid, but even I can see that you've been doing your best by Dahlia and Netta. For that alone, I'd help you."

I'm touched and surprised to find I have people in my corner. Dahlia always said I had more friends at home than I realize, and maybe she's right. The people in this town haven't always disliked me. There was a time that Cleo Boucher, orphaned so young, was the delight of all the grannies and grandpas in this little town. It wasn't until the drama with Ben and Vincent that they turned against me. Maybe I should forgive them. After all, they had no knowledge of my reasons for any of it. When it really comes down to it, who can blame them? Certainly not me. And Dahlia understood this and loved them, and me, despite it all.

Ben is a silent presence at my hip, listening but staying out of a conversation he disapproves of. He doesn't stop me when I ask the ladies to talk to their families and friends about the goings-on in Shaconage. If anyone can find out, it's the gossips of this town.

28

After the rental company picked up the Jeep, Ben drove me to the hospital to see Dahlia. When we arrive, I go straight to Dahlia's room while Ben heads to the nurse's station to ask someone to call the doctor down. I don't know what I was expecting. She looks the same, though the bruising on her face has faded to a dull yellow. I kneel next to her and take her hand in mine.

"Dahlia. It's me, Cleo. Can you hear me?" I wait, hoping for signs my words have reached the seemingly lost recesses of her mind. When there's no response, I sigh but continue to hold her hand.

It's just Dahlia and me for a while, and I take my time telling her my worries, my fears, and how much I love her. When I get to the topic of Ben, I hesitate. What if he overhears me talking about him from the hall? For one, I may never recover from the embarrassment. Second, If Ben were to hear me bare my soul to Dahlia, I'd be vulnerable, completely exposed. But I need to talk to Dahlia about how I'm feeling, even if she can't respond with advice.

Eager to avoid exposure, I leave my spot on the floor to climb into the bed with her, snuggling in close, breathing in her scent, as I continue to hold her hand in mine. My heart aches when it's not bergamot and jasmine I smell, but the sterile scent of hospital soap and dried blood. I do my best to ignore it and lay my head on her shoulder, so much thinner than I remember it.

For a moment, I don't say much at all. Holding her hand, I rest my head on her shoulder and gaze out the window.. The sky is darkening, storm clouds gathering, and I frown. It'll be raining soon. I clear my throat, finding it thick and unsure.

"Dahlia, I have so many questions. I wish you would wake up and tell me the answers. I was surprised that you cleaned out my room. My paintings are gone too. I thought you liked them." Tears forming in the corners of my eyes, I rub small circles on her hand as I continue to talk. I struggle to keep them from falling.

"I've been gone a while, a long time. I know that. But I'm hurt. It's like you just...erased me." The ache has grown now, enveloping me and twisting me around, upside down. "I've been staying at the house, taking care of your plants and chickens. They're fine, don't worry."

At this point, I'm not sure I should mention what's been going on while she's been inpatient here. I don't want to impede her healing, but who can I talk to if not her?

I pick at the buttons on the shoulder of her night-gown as I consider what I want to tell her. About me. About Ben. About the stalker. "It's hard without you here, especially when I need your guidance more than ever." I shift in the bed, squeeze her hand, and continue. "I moved into Ben's place today. Oh, not romantically. It was out of self-preservation. I'm being stalked. Of course, you must have suspected as much. Why didn't you just tell me about the letters, Dahlia? I could have handled it." The last comes out so quietly, I'm sure she wouldn't have heard it even if she were awake.

"He kissed me. He touched my scars, Dee. He ran his fingers over them like they—I—are precious. It was painful. Not physically, you understand, but emotionally. I have been alone for so long, so afraid to let anyone in. I'm...I'm scared, Granny." At that, the tears fall in a torrent. My tears turn to sobs, and soon, I'm choking on them.

I let myself cry for what feels like hours when I hear footsteps approaching the door, the muffled voices of Ben and another, softer voice drifting toward us. With my free hand, I wipe furiously at the back of my eyelids, though I know the evidence will be there still. I'm just pulling myself up when I feel it. In shock, I freeze, hopeful and scared.

She squeezed my hand.

Red-faced and slack-jawed is how they find me seconds later. Did she communicate with me, comfort me, or was it only reflex that caused her hand to squeeze mine? Ben's hand on my shoulder pulls me back to reality.

"Everything okay?"

"She...She squeezed my hand, Ben. She's..." I look back at Ben, then the woman beside him, and smile. "She's still in there." Ben turns to the woman, who is nodding her head.

She extends her hand, and I take it. "Hi, Cleo. I'm Dr. Panakar. We spoke on the phone. As I told you before, Dahlia has started to make some progress. For a while, it seemed recovery was unlikely. But, in the last couple of days, we've begun to see early signs that she could make a recovery. How much of a recovery is unknown at this point." She pauses, taking Dahlia's free hand in hers to check her pulse. She tucks the hand back under the cover before turning to me again. "I can't give you false hope. I won't do that. It's hard to know if she'll continue to make gains in her recovery. We are hopeful, and we're doing everything we can to make it happen."

"So it's a good sign that she squeezed my hand?"

"Yes, it is. I say that because she has advanced beyond simply squeezing a person's hand. When we've worked with her, we've noticed she's started to squeeze our hand when we ask her to. Which means she is hearing us. For now, that's all we have. If, and when, she begins to mumble or opens her eyes, you'll be the first to know."

"That makes sense, I guess. I was telling Dahlia some things and became emotional. I don't know if she was trying to let me know she heard me or not, but it was comforting all the same."

"It's difficult to know for sure."

We talk with Dr. Panakar for a few minutes longer before she leaves to check in on other patients. Dahlia doesn't squeeze my hand again, but I try not to let it get to me. She will get better. It's only a matter of time.

29

Light filters through the shades in Ben's guest room, prompting me to start the day. I've already had three missed calls and a snoozed alarm that I ignored without guilt. For the first time since I got home, I slept all night. Whether this was due to Dahlia's improvement or, perhaps, feeling safer at Ben's, is up for debate.

Three raps sound against the front door downstairs, and I listen to Ben's boots plod down the staircase. Groggy, I sit up and run my fingers through my long blonde hair. The bangs are growing out, and unless I get to a salon soon, they'll be nothing but a nuisance by next week. With a groan, I lean over the side of the bed and catch my satchel with a finger, pulling it up and into my lap.

Quickly now, I rummage until I find a bobby pin. I sigh with relief once I've pinned my bangs out of the way, and I've pulled the rest into a loose ponytail. I grab a pair of purple Nike running shorts from a drawer. I've just pulled a shirt over my head when Ben knocks on the door.

"Uh, Cleo. Can you come out here for a sec?"

A quick glance in the mirror tells me I'm presentable, though I'd prefer to brush my teeth first.

"Be right out." I step into the bathroom and run a toothbrush over my teeth and gargle mouthwash before running back into the bedroom to grab my phone.

Huh. Three missed calls from Tate. I open the messages to see several requests that I call him. As I open the bedroom door, respond to them. I hit send, turning expectantly toward the couch where Ben is seated.

And next to him, sits Tate. My easy smile morphs into a grin just as I hear his phone receive my text. "Oh, my god. Tate! What are you doing here?"

He stands and crosses the room, taking me into his arms. He kisses the top of my head, and my heart melts into a puddle on the floor. It is so easy to be loved by Tate. He pulls back to look me in the eye.

"I've been calling you all morning. I got worried after our last call and flew in last night. This morning, I drove to the address you gave me but was surprised—and worried—when you weren't home. Cleo, the place looks like a crime scene! Caution tape covered the whole place, and then you weren't answering your phone..." He trails off and frowns. In the melee yesterday, I forgot to fill him in. I put my hand on his arm, half to comfort, the other to apologize.

"Oh, Tate. I'm so sorry. Things got complicated and messy yesterday. Someone broke in at the house and threw a brick through the Jeep window. I'm staying here now. For safety." I tack the last part on, though I'm not sure why I feel the need. Tate has no reason to be jealous of Ben, does he? I make eye contact with Ben over Tate's head. He holds my gaze, his own unreadable. He clears his throat.

Tate steps away from me and glances over at Ben with a polite smile. I can't tell his own feelings about Ben. He seems unbothered. And why shouldn't he be? He doesn't know my history with Ben, only that I was briefly married to his brother.

That's a conversation that will eventually need to happen. And if Tate and I decide to take our friendship to the next level, he'll need to know the full truth. I may have promised Vincent I wouldn't talk about our marriage with Ben, but I can't do that to someone I'd start a lifetime with.

Tate smiles at Ben and puts his arm around me. "Thank you for taking care of my girl. I know I don't have to tell you how special she is. I would have come sooner if she hadn't mentioned her brother-in-law was the sheriff. When she told me you were here, Mr. DeMarco, I felt much more at ease. I knew I'd find her if I came to the sheriff's office." He laughs. "I just didn't expect to find her in the actual building."

I give an awkward laugh at that, desperate to ease some of the tension I feel in the air, though Tate appears oblivious.

While it's true that Ben is technically my brother-in-law, it feels like a gut punch to hear it said aloud. What the hell am I thinking, letting him kiss me, touch me? I look away from his probing gaze, my lips pressed into a tight, thin line to hide the tremble that teeters there.

"Well, that's what family is for. Am I right, Cleo?" Ben's sarcasm is lost on Tate, who continues to beam from beside me. But I know better. He wasn't feeling brotherly toward me yesterday when he was threatening to haul me into bed like a caveman at the mere mention of Tate's name.

When I don't respond, he gives me a grin that makes my gut curl. A grin I can only describe as wicked. *Shit.* He picks up his phone from the coffee table and starts toward the stairs.

"See y'all later. I need to get to work now." He disappears down the stairs, and I don't breathe until I hear the door slam shut below.

My phone pings, alerting me of a text, and I open it.

"Great, okay. I say we get some breakfast. I saw a diner on my way to the sheriff's office this morning." Tate continues to talk, but I don't hear a thing.

I'm too busy staring at my phone, reading Ben's text over and over again.

I told you not to say his name again.

Like being released from a net, butterflies flit through my stomach, lifting me off my feet. My cheeks flush with excitement—and dread—at the thought of seeing Ben again tonight. What if he follows through on his threat from yesterday? More than that, do I want him to?

We find seats easily at Pop's Diner. We aren't there long before patrons come by, introducing themselves to Tate. Then the questions start.

"Is this your boyfriend, Cleo?"

"What brings you to Shaconage, Tate?"

"How do you know our Cleo?"

"Have you been to see Dahlia, Tate?"

"Has Bennett met him?" That one gets me a funny look from Tate. He doesn't press me on it, and I don't offer any explanation, even after the fifth person asks about Ben.

It's funny, really, how quickly the tide changes. Just days ago, no one would speak to me in public. Thanks to the rumor mill—and the power of group think—I'm no longer persona non grata. I'm back to being "Our Cleo" and each and every one of them is sizing Tate up, looking for defects among the charm.

Finally, the last of them trickle out the door, leaving Tate both stunned and delighted.

"You didn't tell me how wonderful everyone is here, Cleo. I don't know how you ever left this place, honestly."

I laugh at that and shake my head. As an outsider, I'm sure the tight-knit community seems charming and even enviable. Those of us lucky enough to grow up here know the sweetness comes with thorns.

"So, what would you like to do today? The sky's the

limit." I'm feeling caged and need to get away from the apartment, the hospital, and the well-meaning neighbors...if only for a while.

So when Tate suggests we go for a hike, I jump on it. A quick hike to the falls is just the distraction I need right now. Besides, I've only raved about the Smokies to Tate for ten years. It's about time he sees what the fuss is about.

Agreeing on a meet up at noon, we go our separate ways. On the walk back to Ben's place, I call Netta. As expected, she was waiting by the phone for news about Dahlia's condition. When she has the whole of it, she ends our call abruptly. I can only laugh when she says she is heading back to Dahlia's side. I never expected any less. Closer than sisters, I grew up convinced they were twins separated at birth.

At the apartment, I quickly gather a few supplies for our hike. I pull a backpack out of my suitcase and fill it with a first aid kit, sandwiches wrapped in plastic to deter bears, and water bottles. On my way out the door, I grab my raincoat, sunscreen, and hat. Satisfied I have the basics, I pull the door tight and confirm it's locked before hurrying to the inn.

If we had the Jeep, we could go farther up into the mountain to a less touristy spot, but we'll have to settle for a kid-friendly hike to the falls. Tate rented a Hybrid sedan. And while I can appreciate his efforts to protect the environment, the little thing isn't going to be tough enough to go where I'd really like to.

Ever conscious of the dangers we're facing, I send a

quick text to Ben and Macy to say that I'm headed out with Tate for a day hike at Abram's Falls. In total, we'll hike about ten miles. Just enough of a hike to get away from the noise in Shaconage, but short enough to ensure we're home for dinner.

30

ahlia was the one who taught me to hike. If I went on hikes with my parents, I was too young for any lasting memories of those experiences to linger. There are no photos, so I can only assume my parents weren't the hiker type. But Dahlia was.

It's baffling to think, but Dahlia took me on twenty-, sometimes thirty-, mile hikes in the summers as a child. We packed our gear in oversized hiking packs and hit the trail just as soon as school let out for summer. We'd be gone for days at a time, coming home to find piles of mail on the front porch and an answering machine full of messages. I was in Brownies at her insistence. Devotion to community and family had always been important to Dahlia.

Not only was she convinced I needed survival skills, but she also felt it was her duty to teach me about the mountains, about nature. Dahlia's grandfather might have founded the town we live in, but he only survived those first years because he fell in love with a Cherokee woman who taught him how.

Dahlia is proud of her native heritage, though by the time she was born, there was little left in the bloodline. And certainly, by the time I was born, all traces were gone completely. Despite this, Dahlia has a love and affinity for the land that can only be attributed to the nurturing of her native ancestors.

When I was a child, she often educated me on the medicinal uses of plants. Her father had been considered a medicine man. More often than not, women and men who couldn't afford the cost of the doctor in town would darken Grandpa Tom's door for treatment. Equally benevolent and a businessman, he traded care for money but also accepted eggs, vegetables, canned goods, and the occasional favor. Dahlia has continued to cultivate the herbs he planted, babying them in a way I've never quite understood.

For my part, I remember sitting on the stoop, listening to Dahlia name the plants and their uses while she weeded and harvested them.

"Cleo, this one here is echinacea. It's a weed, really, but it's good for colds and fevers. That's why we grow them out here, with the herbs. Do you remember when you had that fever in February?" It was the year I turned seven. I'm small on the steps, watching her with serious eyes. My honey-blonde hair has lightened in the summer heat and lies unbound on my bony shoulders.

"I made you tea from it. It's important you learn this, Cleo. It's our family legacy." A woven basket is at her side, overflowing with clipped flowers and herbs I know will soon

hang to dry in the sunroom. It is one of my favorite rooms in the house. I often go there to be alone and sniff sachets of lavender.

"Cleo, are you listening?" I nod, and she continues, "If you get a deep cut and you need to go to the hospital, what should you use?" I frown and stare at my sneakers. Dahlia told me last week, but I don't remember now.

"Chamomile?" I know it's the wrong choice, but it's the only herb that comes to mind. Dahlia shakes her head with a sigh and sits back from her crouched position on the ground.

"Paprika, darling. Paprika. Pack it in the wound until you can get help. It will staunch the bleeding."

As quickly as the memory came, it's gone. Tate is driving, so I let myself relax and take in the scenery that's haunted my dreams for the last decade.

I'm not surprised when Tate handles the hike like a pro. He's notorious for his gym sessions, sometimes going twice a day. He invited me on occasion, but I prefer to run outdoors, even in the Arizona heat. Thankfully, this hike is flatter than my typical choice, or I might have lagged. I don't think I've run once since I got home.

It rained yesterday, and if the darkening skies are any indication, it will rain again today. I'm not worried. We are wearing sturdy hiking shoes, and we packed raincoats. If anything, the threat of rain is a godsend. We have the trail mostly to ourselves.

The trees here inspired me to become an artist. Those

hikes with Dahlia inevitably ended with me sitting at the base of a tree, sketching cones and pine needles. Dahlia never rushed me. When you're a seventy-plus grandma raising a child, timelines don't matter as much as when you're young, on a deadline, and trying to fit an entire vacation into a week's time. It's not lost on me how lucky I was to have had those experiences.

Sometimes, Macy came with us because her mom, a single parent, rarely took vacation time. Though my best friend, Macy wasn't as big a fan of the national park as I was. She did, however, like to take photos. So, while I sat and sketched, she took photos of other hikers we met, of Dahlia, and of me. Even as a child, she had skill, though I didn't recognize it at the time.

Most of the photos from my childhood were taken by Macy. Dahlia wasn't much for documenting life in pictures. She did, of course, buy my school photos and yearbooks, but she took few herself. Instead, Dahlia wrote diaries and letters every day of her life.

The forest is quiet, the sounds of birds the only thing to break the silence. Tate and I don't talk, but he smiles at me often, sending little tendrils of excitement through me. But with that excitement comes confusion and guilt. I can't help but feel like I've betrayed him by kissing Ben. *Am I betraying Ben by being here with him?*

Neither Tate nor Ben has blatantly said they have feelings for me nor that they want to start a relationship. Realistically, I know I have done nothing wrong. Yet previous experiences tell me that doesn't matter. Someone will inevitably be hurt—even if that someone ends up being me.

Roaring, the waterfall announces its presence long before we see it. Abram's Falls was named for a Cherokee chief long before my ancestors and others settled in this area. The cry of the water hitting rock is the closest thing the woods have to a war cry these days. I close my eyes and take it in, the moisture in the air greeting me like a soft kiss.

Feeling lighter than I have in days, I smile at Tate, motioning him to take a seat with me on a rock near the base of the falls. I take off the backpack and pull out our water bottles and sandwiches. Between bites, I tell him bits and pieces of history.

"These mountains are called The Smokies because of the way the fog sits on them. The Cherokee called them Shaconage. That's where the name of our town came from. When my great-grandfather settled here, he named it for the Cherokee word."

I don't tell him how I dream of home, how Arizona will never be what I need. Gone thirteen years and yet the moment I returned, it was as if a missing puzzle piece was finally uncovered and locked into place. Blood will win out, as they say. And this place roars in mine.

"Was your grandfather Cherokee, then?" Tate is lying on his side on the rock. He loves history, so I know for a fact his interest is genuine.

"No, but his wife was. Her name was Tanasi. Another Cherokee word white settlers butchered. You might recognize it. Tanasi. Tennessee. They are very similar."

"Wait. Isn't that your middle name?"

"Yes. My parents named me after her, at least partially. Cleo is for my mom's aunt." At that, my smile drops. My mom's people are long gone, too. It truly is only Dahlia and me now.

"But your last name is…French?"

"It's a French name, yes. It means 'butcher,' though I don't know of any ancestors who were in that profession. They must have been at some point, I suppose. Unless, of course, it was a war name. Regardless of origin, my ancestors settled long ago in Pennsylvania. I think it was sometime in the 1700s, though Dahlia would know more about that than me. She married into the Boucher family when my Grandpa Moses Boucher moved near Shaconage. He took one look at her and was a goner, or so the story goes."

I never met Grandpa Moses. He, like my parents and grandparents, died young, leaving his young widow to raise Grandpa Joe on her own. Then, Grandpa Joe had my dad, Kent.

Our family had a habit of only having one child, though I don't think this was done purposely. Somehow, it seemed there was only one child that made it to adulthood. My parents wanted to give me siblings, and I had the best sister in Cecily. According to Dahlia, they planned to have another, a third child, but that was taken from them. Instead, I carry on the one-living child legacy of my family.

Tears threaten to spill, but I'm tired of crying. I don't want to ruin this time with Tate. Instead, I unlace my boots and pull them off before jumping to my feet. Tate's eyes go wide when I shimmy out of my shorts. I laugh at his expression as I toss them aside. I leave my shirt, conscious as ever of the scars across my belly.

With one last look at him, I dive into the water, staying under just long enough to feel the burn in my lungs before surfacing. When I come up, Tate is standing on the rock, worry lines etched into the beautiful skin above his brow. His face clears when he sees me.

"You coming?" He looks over at my discarded shoes and shorts before turning back to me with a big grin. Soon, we're laughing and splashing in the water together like a couple of kids. I dare him to a race under the falls, which, surprisingly, he wins. When we come up for air, he pulls me close under the spray and kisses me.

Eyes sparkling, he pulls back from me, his hold on me easy and sweet. I look up into his eyes, and I know, without a doubt, that loving Tate would be so easy, so right. He'd never hurt me. He wouldn't leave me. And no matter what secrets I hold, he'd keep them. I know he'd keep them forever. I'm mesmerized, engulfed. So, when he finally speaks, I jump at the intrusion of words within the magic of it.

"Cleo, I need you to understand how I feel. Even though I've tried to be reasonable, to be your friend without expectations, I can't ignore it anymore. I adore you." I'm caught in the fire I see in his eyes, mesmerized like a moth drawn to a flame. When I don't respond, he says, more quietly, "I love you, Cleo."

Speechless, I simply raise my hand, dripping with water, to caress his face. His eyes follow the movement of my hand before reconnecting with my gaze. Without a word, I lean in and touch his lips with mine.

31

s soon as we leave the national park, my phone
starts to ping with notifications. While we
were disconnected, the gossip mill of
Shaconage was busy. One by one, I forward their
messages to Ben.

> Cleo, I spoke to Robert over at the
> hardware store. He said he saw Devin
> Mathews and Dahlia get into a heated
> argument over light bulbs the week
> before she was attacked. He had to
> make Devin leave the store.

It seems our mailman, John, saw Mark Jeffers at
Dahlia's house one afternoon when Dahlia wasn't home.
He didn't speak to Jeffers but is certain it was him. I'm
not surprised by this information, as both Jeffers and
Mathews have confirmed recent dealings with Dahlia.
Devin said himself he tried to get information about me
from Dahlia and failed.

When I get back to the apartment, my replacement

175

rental car is waiting for me. Instead of a Jeep, a Nissan Rogue was the only SUV available this time. I collect the keys from Deputy Franks and throw a wave toward Ben when he calls my name. I exit the building, my steps quick as I hurry to key in the code for the apartment. Once inside, I take the stairs two at a time and lock myself in the guest room just as I hear Ben tear into the apartment.

I ignore his knock on the door and start a shower instead. When he hears the water start, he quiets. After a moment, I hear him exit the apartment. I release the breath I was holding and turn to the shower, stepping in and forgetting everything for a while.

When I'm dry and dressed, I send a quick text to Tate to check in about dinner. On a project deadline, he begs off but invites me over for late drinks. I chew my lip and consider the implications. Late drinks are an invitation for more. Even I know that. I write several responses, varying from "Yes" to "I'm not sure it's a good idea." In the end, I don't respond at all. Instead, I pack a change of clothes and my sketchbook. With one last look around the room, I grab the keys and let myself out. In the rearview, I watch as both the sheriff's office and the inn where Tate waits grow smaller and smaller before they disappear completely.

Netta is surprised but pleased to see me when I arrive at the hospital. Though the rules clearly prohibit two overnight guests, an exception is granted, and an additional cot and bedding are wheeled in. While Netta fusses with the bedding, I send a text to Ben.

"Don't wait up. I won't be in tonight." I'm relieved to put off the confrontation until tomorrow. I'm aware it's cowardly to use Dahlia as a shield, but Ben's intensity these last few days terrifies me. But more than that, it excites me. With everything that's between us, do I really want to throw away an opportunity to have a normal and healthy relationship with Tate for a "maybe" with Ben? No, it's best to walk away while I still have a chance.

Tate, as usual, doesn't bat an eye when I tell him I'm staying with Dahlia tonight. We agree to meet for breakfast tomorrow at the diner.

I don't hear from Ben for hours, then I receive a simple "Ok."

In the end, staying with Dahlia at the hospital is best. Around nine, just as we are settling into sleep, Dahlia Boucher opens her eyes.

32

I wake up to texts from Ben, which I ignore. The last thing I want to do today is have a "what is this" discussion with him, though I know I can't put it off forever. The same conversation needs to be had with Tate, and I'm drained just thinking about it.

In the afternoon, Dr. Panakar drops in to reassess Dahlia, who has opened her eyes twice this morning. She has made eye contact with me but doesn't stay awake for long. She has said nothing, but I hope that is temporary.

I texted Tate early this morning, and he agreed we should push our breakfast date to dinner. I haven't taken a break to call Ben, but I'm not worried. He'll be as thrilled as the rest of us to hear the news.

Macy, understandably, wanted to come over first thing, but Dr. Panakar vetoed additional visitors to avoid overstimulation. For now, Dahlia's limited to visits from Netta and me. While I know she needs rest and time, I can't help but hope she gives us a name soon. Now that she's awake, it's only a matter of time. Soon, we'll put this to rest forever.

Exhausted, Dahlia sleeps most of the afternoon. When evening comes, I consider canceling dinner with Tate, but Netta shoos me out. What good am I when Dahlia is asleep? When put like that, I have little argument. Besides, a change of clothes and a shower would do me well.

The drive back to Shaconage is quick and uneventful. Several townspeople wave at me as I drive in, and I'm not a bit surprised to find myself smiling back at them. Home isn't so bad once I was taken off the "Public Enemy #1" list.

Coward that I am, I let out a sigh of relief when I pull in to find Ben's truck missing from the lot. One problem at a time. And Lord knows, Ben's a problem I'm not ready to address.

Bennett DeMarco was always a passionate kid, regardless of whether that was making a tackle on the football field or arguing theology with Pastor Lincoln. Ben just didn't know how to quit. And it was fascinating, it really was. At least, it's fascinating until you find your-self on the other end of that intensity. Then, well, it's something else entirely. That's not to say I'm afraid he'll hurt me. No, it's more than that. I'm terrified that Ben DeMarco will consume me completely, leaving me nothing but a lifeless and empty shell.

I shake those grim thoughts off, thinking of Tate's sweet face, and hurry through the motions of showering and dressing for dinner. On my way out, I search for Ben's truck, but again, he's not there.

I pull my phone from my bag and open his texts, scrolling through the last ones I received—the ones I purposefully marked read but ignored.

> Re-read some of those letters, and it doesn't make sense. Will fill you in later.

> Call me. It's important.

> Are you still with that guy? I need to talk to you about the letters. I found some info.

I notice three missed calls. Then nothing.

No one is on the sidewalk outside the apartment, so I quickly key in his number and hit send. I get his voicemail. Instead of leaving a message, I send a quick text.

> Ben, sorry for not getting back to you. I was with Dahlia. Can you call me back?

I dart a glance at the diner before turning back to enter the station. Both Ben and Deputy Franks are out, but the part-time receptionist, Leah, is seated behind the front desk.

"Cleo, I haven't seen you in ages!" She stands to give me a hug, and for once, I don't have to bend down. Leah is, somehow, taller than me. She smells like vanilla and sugar cookies, which somehow doesn't seem out of place in the summer heat. Dressed in jeans and a polo with the sheriff's department logo, her long brown hair is twisted into a fishtail braid, reminding me of long-ago days on the playground. Her smile is infectious, leading me to momentarily forget my purpose.

"Leah, I had no idea you were working here. Ben never mentioned it." I roll my eyes and we both laugh. "How are you? Have you been back in town long?" Like me, Leah left town shortly after high school, though for different reasons. Leah wasn't running from her past. She had a full ride to the University of Tennessee and moved to Knoxville.

"Home is home." She shrugs as if that says everything, and honestly, it kind of does. She looks at me expectantly, and I flush when I realize she's asked me a question.

"Uh, what? Sorry, it's been...crazy."

At that, she sobers, nodding. "Yes, I heard about Dahlia. Well, you know how it is. We all did." She shrugs, clearly uncomfortable with being thought a gossip.

"It's fine, really. I'm glad to know so many people care about her. She's made some big improvements, so we're hopeful." Tears prick the corners of my eyes, threatening to spill over.

Leah lays a comforting hand on my shoulder. "That's great to hear, Cleo. Wonderful even."

Embarrassed and trying to avoid a waterfall of tears, I break eye contact and peer farther into the office. As I thought, no one else is there. I wipe my eyes and clear my throat. She hands me a tissue, and I take my time, making sure I feel collected before I make eye contact again.

"Have you seen Ben? We're playing phone tag, and I really need to talk to him."

She shakes her head. "He ran out of here early this morning. Said he needed to look into something and would be back later. About an hour ago, Franks told me Ben wouldn't be back in today." She skims the calendar on the desk before looking back up apologetically. "There's nothing on the calendar for today. Court is on Mondays, and he doesn't have any lunches scheduled either." She clicks her tongue and turns toward the back of the room where Ben's office sits. She walks into it and rummages through the pile of papers on his desk for a moment before returning empty-handed. "Sorry, nothing there either. I could call him if you'd like." She puts a hand on the receiver, ready to pick it up.

"No, don't bother him." I look at my watch and grimace. *Shit.* "I'm late for dinner, anyway. I better get over to the diner before my date thinks I stood him up." A sparkle comes into her eyes at the mention of my date. I give her a sly grin as I back out the door, my hands up.

"Wait, Cleo!"

I don't stop moving; instead, I laugh and jog down the street toward Pop's. The gossip mill will be busy tonight. The smile lingers, teasing the corners of my mouth. That same smile blossoms when I catch sight of familiar blond curls in a corner booth.

33

Saying goodbye is never a simple thing. When I first came back to Shaconage, I imagined the goodbye I'd face, the one that would rip me in two, would be with Dahlia. Never, in my wildest dreams, would I have imagined coming back here would lead to the end of Tate and me. Of whatever this thing was between the two of us.

He left me over an hour ago, but I'm frozen here, unable to leave this booth. Just yesterday, we were kissing under a waterfall, for God's sake. More than that, he'd told me he loved me. He said he *adores* me. I turn our conversation over and over in my head, piecing it together, my anxiety turning to grief.

"I'm not taking back what I said. I love you, Cleo. I always have, and I think I always will. But you have unfinished business here. I'd be a fool to start something with you, knowing your heart isn't ready, when it isn't free."

I protested. Of course, my heart is free, there's no one. Despite my protests, I knew he was right. As much as I want Tate, I can't seem to let go of my feelings for Ben. And I hate myself for it.

"At first, when Ben's name was mentioned, I thought it was sweet that people wanted to know his opinion about the two of us. A protective brother-in-law is a good thing, right? I could be a bad guy for you. I get it. But then, imagine my shock when the innkeeper told me that you had a history with Ben. Once I got the full story—offered up to me on a silver platter—everything made sense."

"You've got it wrong, Tate. Ben and I—we're all wrong for each other. There's nothing to worry about."

"Can you tell me, honestly, that there's been nothing between the two of you since you came back?"

"I—" My cheeks fill with color, my throat with tears. "He's not you. You make me feel safe. He doesn't. He makes me feel..."

"He makes you feel what, Cleo?" He gives the hand he's holding a squeeze, and I press my eyes closed, desperate to erase the look I find in his.

I feel weak, unmoored. Tate has been my rock for so many years. Without him, I'm not sure I can face the dangers that lurk here. I give myself a shake. Tate did not abandon me. To his credit, he has promised to remain my financial planner. As my friend, he is available for anything I need. Anything, that is, except him.

My phone chirps with an incoming text. With movements that feel leaden, I pull the phone from my bag and open messages.

> We need to talk right now. Where
> are you?

It's from Ben, and I frown, anxiety catapulting me out of the booth and onto my feet. I throw cash onto the table and text him back, typing as I rush to the door.

> Where are you? OMW to your place now.

He types several times before stopping without replying at all. I put my phone in my pocket and jog the rest of the way to the apartment. I stutter to a stop when I see his truck outside. The lights upstairs are dark, and the shades drawn, so I walk over to the station and peer inside. The lights are dimmed in there as well. Stepping back, I glance up at the apartment windows again just in time to see a light come on. I key in the code and take the stairs two at a time.

A single lamp illuminates the living room, and I can't help the gasp that escapes when I see Ben in the shadows. "Oh my god, Ben. I didn't see you there." I laugh, my hand over my heart, clutching my T-shirt tightly between my fingertips.

He doesn't respond. He doesn't move. Almost like a statue, he remains seated, bent at the waist, staring at a piece of paper in his hand. His knuckles are white, almost as pale as the paper in them. The other hand is in his hair, no longer neat and tidy but wild.

I inch toward him, hoping when I get to him, I can somehow snap him out of whatever funk he's in. The only sound in the room is the scuff of my Nikes on the floor, each squeak impossibly loud in the otherwise tomb-like space.

When I'm close, I kneel next to him and put my hand on his knee. He flinches at the contact but doesn't speak. My own voice is strained, creaking open like a rusty gate as I break the silence.

"Ben, talk to me. What's going on?" I take his hand in mine and squeeze it. He looks at me, his gaze feral and searching. When he finally speaks, it's low and dangerous, each word moving me from compassionate to defensive.

"I pulled the hospital records from the accident that killed Vincent. I reviewed the records for Jeffers and Vincent, which we can talk about later. But I also pulled yours, Cleo. Can you guess what I found there?"

Dropping his hand, I jump to my feet, a strangled gasp leaving me. I don't make eye contact with him. I can't. I'm afraid—more afraid than I've been since I got here, possibly more than I've been in my entire life. My chest contracts, and I can feel myself breaking. I shake my head, though, as an answer or a denial that the conversation is occurring is unclear to me.

My steps are swift as I make my escape, my eyes on the stairs. I can't have this conversation. I promised Vincent I would keep the secret. But, more than that, once Ben knows, I'm defenseless. I hear Ben's footsteps following me and increase my pace. My right foot hits the first step before I'm yanked back into his chest. I'm too scared to move, so I don't. My breath is coming in hard pants, anxiety and grief gripping me in a tight fist.

I don't see his face, and I'm glad he can't see mine, as he continues.

"Imagine my surprise to find out you were pregnant when you married Vincent. When I saw the report, I was heartbroken for you and for Vincent, but also for myself and my parents, who lost another piece of him."

A soft cry leaves me, tears pricking my eyes. "Ben, please." My voice is a whisper.

"But then—and this is the damnedest thing—I read the rest of the report. What I want to know, Cleo, is when, exactly, were you going to tell me about my child?"

34

How do I explain to my dead child's father that I never intended to tell him about what we lost? It's not because he didn't deserve to know but more, he didn't deserve the pain. If Vincent had survived, the pain of that loss would have been shared between the two of us. When Ben left, he didn't just leave me. He left the baby, too, whether he knew about it or not.

At least, that's how I used to feel. Now I'm not so sure. I never intended to come back here. I certainly never intended to see or speak to Ben again. The loss we shared and faced was just too huge to ever consider a space in this world where we could reconcile, where we could move forward together.

With shaky hands, I reach up and remove his from where they are gripping my shoulders, and slowly turn to face him. The pain I feel is reflected in his eyes. Tears well up and spill over as I take him in, the grief he's feeling so raw and new. I take an uneven breath and wet my lips.

"I wasn't going to tell you."

He starts at that and I see anger seep into the grief. His hands lift and grip me tight, holding me still before him. Before he can comment, I start again.

"I wasn't going to tell you because Vincent and I agreed not to tell anyone about the baby for a while, and once he and the baby were gone, I kept the secret."

"Is it mine?" His whisper, so quiet and exposed, guts me.

"Yes." A tear escapes to roll down my cheek and into the crease between my lips. I taste the salt but ignore it, holding Ben's gaze. His grip tightens on me still. He doesn't seem aware he's squeezing me, and I wonder if I'll bruise tomorrow. I don't bring it up, anxious to get everything out now that the bottle has been uncorked.

"Yes, the baby was yours. I found out right after you left."

"Why didn't you tell me—wait, did Vincent know it was my baby?" Suddenly suspicious, he leans back and peers into my eyes, searching them as if he can detect insincerity there.

I sigh and look at my feet. I can feel my shoulders hunch, and I force myself to meet his gaze again.

"Yes, Vincent knew it was your baby. That's how it all happened. He—I—You—" I stop and take a deep breath. "I tried to call you...at basic training. But they wouldn't let me talk to you. You left me, Ben. You left." My face is hot and my vision blurs as the tears fall in a torrent. I never really let myself cry about it. Oh, I cried plenty after the accident, for Vincent and the baby, but I never really grieved the loss of Ben. There was never time, really, before the wedding. And after...well, there was bigger pain.

"You left me, and I didn't know what to do. I was eighteen years old. This is a small town that you know would eat me alive the moment they knew I was pregnant and alone." My voice softens when I start to talk about Vincent, and Ben must notice because his grip loosens slightly, but he doesn't let go.

"I sought Vincent out. I thought maybe he could help me get in touch with you or help me leave for a while, at least until I could have the baby and figure things out." I smile, remembering him. "It was Vincent's idea. He asked me to marry him." I lift my arms and Ben releases me. I take his face in my hands. "You need to know this, so please listen."

He nods and doesn't speak.

"I loved you, Ben. More than anything in this world, I loved you. When you left, it destroyed me." His face jerks under my hands, but he doesn't interrupt me. I rub my thumbs softly on his cheeks, digging deep to find the strength to continue.

"When I found out I was pregnant, I found a new purpose. There was this little baby that needed me, and I would have done anything." My voice breaks, and I stop, taking a moment to collect myself before speaking again. "I would have done whatever it took to make sure our child was accepted here, that he or she had a solid family —the kind I lost, but the sort I knew you had. So, when Vincent asked me to marry him, I said yes."

Slowly, I trace my fingers across his brow, memorizing the lines on his face. The ache is huge, and I'm all too aware that the strides we've made these last days could be obliterated with this revelation.

"But what I need you to know most of all is this: I loved Vincent." I hear him inhale, but to his credit, he doesn't interrupt me. He lets me finish. "I loved Vincent, though not passionately, not in the way I loved you. I loved him—adored him—for his offer, for his excitement about the baby. I loved that he loved our child. And he would have made a great dad. Because that's what he would have been. When I accepted his offer, it was forever. I knew accepting him meant there was no future for you and me, but I did so gladly, with appreciation and affection. Within weeks, I loved him in a way I can't describe. It was real. I need you to know that." With those last words, I drop my gaze and my hands from his face. I stare at his chest instead of him, ready to accept whatever abuse he throws at me.

"I came back."

My head whips back up, our eyes crashing into one another, both shimmering with tears and pain. My lips part in shock. What does he mean, he came back?

"After basic training. I came home. I regretted it all, Cleo. A few weeks away made me realize I needed to see you, to make things right."

"I didn't see you, though. You never came by."

"No, I went home first." He laughs a bit unsteadily. "When I got home, there were wedding coordinators at the house. I came in at the end, but I heard them mention Vincent's name...then yours."

"But why didn't you—"

"I couldn't stand it, Cleo. The whole thing blindsided me and part of me thought you had been seeing him behind my back. It made me a little crazy. I left before my mom saw me and drove straight to your house, ready to confront you, call you out. But when I got there, no one was home. I almost left to find Vincent, but then I looked through the front window and there it was. There was a beautiful wedding gown laid out across the couch and I couldn't face it—couldn't face you. I didn't go back home. I just left."

And then he didn't call or show up for our wedding.

He stops to take my face in his hands, wiping away the tears gathered in the corners of my eyes. I stare up at him, each word splintering my heart into smaller and smaller pieces.

"I wish I had been stronger, Cleo, that I had gone to you and demanded to talk, to know if you loved me or if you wanted him. I've thought about it every day for the last thirteen years. Sometimes, I've been angry with you, but more often than not, I've only ached for you."

He brushes a kiss across my forehead and whispers against my hair. "Don't you see, Cleo? You're it for me."

I'm stunned at his revelation. More than that, I'm afraid. I have no shield to protect me, no reason to remind me to keep my distance from Bennett. He knows everything now. And now that he knows, I'm finding it difficult to keep my emotions bottled. My hands tremble as I pull back from him, trying to extricate myself from his arms, but he doesn't let go.

"Please, Ben...I need some space." I pull at his grip,

but he only tightens it, though not to hurt, only to hold. "Ben. Let me go." Like a moth drawn to a flame, I can only sigh when he closes the remaining distance to place his lips on mine.

I freefall into it, letting myself revel in the sensation of his lips against mine. They move slowly and deliberately, soothing yet building an even deeper ache within me. Needing a closer connection, I put my arms around him and pull him in as close as I can, until I can feel his heart beating against my own.

His lips leave mine to trail across my jaw and down my neck. I arch against him, his feather-soft lips sending me into overdrive. His breath fans across the skin near my neck, and a shudder runs through me. I run my fingers through his hair, overwhelmed by the feelings pouring through and out of me, and into his mouth.

As if in answer to them, he slides his tongue to mine, somehow melding us even closer together. Succumbing to this new sensation, I sway on my feet, my knees weak. This causes me to lose my footing, slipping off the edge of the top step. I break the kiss and grab his shoulders to regain my balance.

I scoot to the side and away from the steps and let go of him. The distance allows me to find a moment of clarity that has me stepping farther away from him. Self-preservation warns me that if I don't put some distance between us, I'll be consumed.

I catch sight of myself in the mirror near the door and nervously run my fingers through my tangled blonde hair. My lips are swollen and bright pink coloring fans over my cheeks. I make eye contact with Ben in the mirror. His dark eyes swallow me, and I know this is far from over. I tug at the corners of my shirt and swallow hard, ready to have the hard conversation—this can't go anywhere.

I blow out a breath and turn, his name on my lips. I've barely a moment before his lips take mine again, urgent and hard. I place my hands on his chest to push him away but, instead, surprise myself by pulling him closer.

He bites my bottom lip, and a wave of desire rolls through me, weakening me once more. Sensing the change, Ben pulls me to him and surprises me further when he picks me up off the floor.

"Ben!" I grope for his shoulders, worried I'm too heavy, that he'll drop me—or worse, fall himself. He doesn't respond. Instead, he walks directly to his bedroom, his long strides making the journey short.

My back hits the mattress, and the words die in my throat when I see the look in his eyes. He follows me onto the bed, straddling my body with his. I swallow, and his eyes follow the movement, growing darker still. He's a storm, swirling all around me, threatening to destroy me from the inside out. And for once, I want to be obliterated.

With a shaky breath, I take the corners of my shirt in my hands and start to peel it from my skin. Warm hands halt my movement, forcing me to meet his gaze. He takes both of my wrists in his hand and pins them above my head.

"I want to be the one to undress you. I want to touch every inch of your body." With his free hand, he skims his fingertips just under my shirt, and I shudder, my body seeking more. I pull at his grip, desperate to touch him, to run my fingers through his thick hair. Instead of loosening, his grip tightens further. "I've thought of nothing else since you got back."

I suck in a breath as his fingers trail higher, his touch so light I feel faint. He brushes my nipple with his thumb before removing his hand completely. I push against him, my body begging him for things I can't articulate. He's an immovable wall above me, my body burning at the pressure of his hips on mine. He releases his grip on my wrists, and when I don't move my hands, he lets go of them.

"Keep your hands above your head, Cleo. Don't move."

I stay still, trapped in his gaze, as he steps away from me. My eyes leave his when he begins to unbutton his shirt, each one stoking the blaze building inside of me. I jerk when he pulls the shirt off, giving me the first glimpse of his broad chest.

"Ben, please." *Please, what, Cleo?* When he pops the button on his jeans, I sit up and reach for him, needing to touch him, to push this along. Now that we've started, I need it—need *him*. I pull at his pants, pushing them down his legs. Pausing, I stroke his thigh and hear him groan above me. I lean forward to press my lips to it. Before I can do the same with his other thigh, strong hands grip me under my arms and haul me up and back onto the bed.

"I said, *don't move*." Quickly now, he pulls my shirt and bra over my head before pushing me down onto the bed. He places my hands above my head once more, and this time, I leave them. With quick movements, he grips my shorts, tearing them from me and tossing them somewhere over his shoulder. My throat goes dry when he loops his thumbs in the band of my underwear and rips them from me.

"You're mine, Cleo. *Mine.*" His head dips, taking one of my nipples into his mouth, sucking it hard and pulling a scream from me. Whatever hold he had on his restraint is gone, and he wastes no time. His fingers find me, and he pushes two into me, harshly, as his mouth continues to suck and bite my nipples.

"Ben, please. I can't—it's too much." My head thrashes from side to side. I'm not lying; it *is* too much. Painful yet so delicious. His fingers are thick inside of me, demanding more and more of me with each thrust.

"We're just getting started, Cleo. I'm not stopping until your body knows it's mine and mine alone."

"It's yours, it's yours, I swear. Please, Ben. I need you inside me." He doesn't respond. Instead, he adds a third finger, causing my body to bow off the bed. My hands go to his shoulders, desperate to find some leverage.

"Hands up, Cleo. Grab the headboard, or I'm cuffing you to it." He adjusts his position, coming alongside me in the bed. I grip the headboard, my eyes wild, my body panting as I stare up at him. He slides his free hand beneath my neck and gives it a gentle squeeze, all while he continues to ram his fingers inside me. "Good girl," he murmurs, his eyes on my lips.

Then his mouth finds mine, and the contrast between the gentle pressure of his mouth and the harsh cadence of his fingers brings tears to my eyes. Higher and higher he pushes me, the pressure building inside of me like a maelstrom. I close my eyes, falling into the sensation, my body close to completion.

Just as I feel myself edging over, Ben removes his hand and mouth from my body, leaving me alone on the bed. I sit up, gasping for breath as I follow his movement across the floor. He watches me from behind hooded eyes as he peels off his boxers before rejoining me. He runs his hands through my long hair before sliding a long finger up my spine to cradle my head in his calloused palms.

With gentle hands, he pulls me into his lap, the action so natural and right my heart swells. I press a kiss to the underside of his jaw and feel him harden beneath me. We both freeze, and I hold my breath, waiting for him to make the next move. I shift and feel the heat of him align perfectly. Seconds, minutes, or hours pass and yet nothing happens. His breath is heavy against my neck, and with each moment, his arousal grows. *Why won't he do something?*

Exhaling a shaky breath, I lean back in order to make eye contact with him. His eyes threaten to burn me down, and for once, I'm not afraid to let him. Holding his gaze, I close the distance between us to place my lips on his.

Instead of deepening the kiss, he pulls back from me, his jaw hard and eyes passionate. His hands tighten around me, and when he speaks, his words sear my soul.

"I'm going to love your body until my touch is the

only one you remember. I'll *ruin you* for anyone else, Cleo."

I open my mouth to speak, but he cuts me off, his lips taking mine in a rough kiss. He adjusts me on his lap, and the tip of him pierces me. He continues to kiss me as he slides slowly inside. Placing my hands on his shoulders, I push away from his lips but remain on his lap. He stills inside of me, questions in his eyes.

With a gasp, I say, "There's been no one else." His fingers clutch me tighter, edging close to pain.

"What did you say?" His words rasp out of him, nearly a whisper.

"I said, there's been no one else since you. You're the only one, Ben. Just you—" The rest is lost when he pushes forward, anchoring himself fully inside of me, his mouth taking mine to quell the scream that tries to rip its way out of me at the sudden invasion.

His hands drag my hips to meet his thrusts, in and out, his mouth never leaving mine. "You're mine, Cleo," he says, ripping his mouth away from mine to push me down onto the bed, his hips never disconnecting from mine. "You've always been mine." He pushes my legs open and places my right leg around his hip as he drills into me.

I do my best to keep up, thrusting my hips at each brutal advance of his. I'm close, each push winding me higher and higher. "I'm—I'm going to come." At that, his grip on my hips becomes bruising, and his next thrust bows me off the bed. "Oh, shit. *Fuck, Ben.*" His mouth closes around my nipple, and I'm gone, my heart stuttering in my chest.

Ben wastes no time, his own movements becoming quicker and more erratic with each thrust. He pulls out of me to flip me onto my stomach. I'm vaguely aware of his actions as he pulls my hips up and back. When he surges into me once more, I shriek from the invasion, so violent, so sweet.

One hand rests on my hip, pulling me into him over and over again, building a rhythm that stokes a new fire within me. His other hand fists into my hair, twisting it: one, two, three times before giving it a soft yank.

"Look at me, Cleo," he says, his voice a hot command on my neck. I force myself to make eye contact with him over my shoulder, my mind reeling at the sensation of his continued thrusts pushing into me, holding me hostage beneath him. "I love you. So damn much."

There's no time to process his words, no time to question or respond. With one last thrust, he orgasms, emptying into me with a groan that rolls through me, sending me tumbling after him.

35

Light tickles the back of my eyelids, dragging me from sleep. I stretch, feeling more rested than I have in weeks. Mid-stretch, I freeze. The revelations from the night before flit through my mind quickly: Tate. Ben's text. The medical records. Kissing Ben.

My hand goes to my mouth, automatically retracing the path of his lips on mine. The feel of his hands around me, on my breasts—.

I sit up quickly, the blanket falling and pooling around my hips. I'm naked. *Holy shit.* I take in the room, noticing for the first time that I'm not in the guest bed. I'm in *Ben's bed.*

Throwing the sheets back, I jump out of the bed, sliding on my T-shirt before dropping to my knees in search of my shorts. I sweep blindly under the bed, my fingers latching onto fabric. I sit back on my heels to study the torn underwear. Memories of the night before dance on replay in my mind. The sound of a door opening somewhere in the apartment has me scrambling to gather my clothing. I make it to the bathroom and close the door just as I hear Ben enter the bedroom.

Through the crack, I watch him stand there, gazing at the bed. After a moment, he places a cup of coffee on the nightstand and leaves the way he came. He never comes to the bathroom, though I know he hears the floor creak as I shift nervously behind the door.

I wait for a moment before tiptoeing out to grab my cell phone where it had fallen from my pocket when he tossed me on the bed last night.

I start a text to Ben.

> Last night was a bad idea.

Before I can send it, though, I get one from him.

> I'm going down to the office for a bit. I'm going to try to catch up with and interview Devin today.

I sigh, relieved I can avoid the awkward morning-after scene. I start to put the phone down when it pings again.

> Oh, and don't try to say last night was a mistake.

And another.

> I'm sure you're freaking out. It's okay. We can talk more tonight.

I take a seat on the toilet and read the texts over and over again. I start and stop several texts, but nothing seems right. I run my hands up and down my thighs and tell myself to breathe. *Everything is going to be okay. It doesn't have to mean anything.* Yet even I know the truth: it means too much.

In the end, I don't reply at all. Instead, I lock the bathroom door and drag myself into the hot shower. I close my eyes and lather, watching the soap go down the drain as I wash him off me.

What else can a girl do when she's feeling over-whelmed but see her mama—or, in my case, make the forty-minute drive to visit with Dahlia? On the way there, I try to process the string of events from the night before but get nowhere. Logically, it was bound to happen. Ben and I have—*had*—unfinished business. Learning about the baby was an emotional bombshell for him and telling him about it was just as hard. It's not hard to believe that those emotions got the best of us and led to sex.

On top of it all, I no longer have Tate as support. And while the feelings I have for Ben are long and compli-cated, they aren't unique. I have feelings just as strong for Tate. More than that, I don't want to lose Tate's friendship. If it were visible, I'm sure my heart would be black and blue from the beatings it has taken in the last twenty-four hours alone.

Wearily, I pull myself from my SUV and take slow, heavy steps toward the entrance of the hospital. Relieved to find the lobby empty of greeters, I turn toward the elevators. Before I walk up to Dahlia's room, I stop by the gift shop for flowers. At the counter, I eye a puzzle book and add it to the total. The flowers are for Dahlia; the book is for Netta.

The door is closed, so I give a quiet knock, hopeful to find Dahlia awake. After a moment, Netta opens it and gives me a huge smile that lights up her entire face. Since Dahlia woke up, it's like life has come back into Netta. For a while there, I worried I was destined to lose two grandmothers at once. I'm relieved that, for now at least, I still have a family.

The blinds are open, and the sun shines through the vertical slats. Netta has positioned Dahlia in just the right spot to avoid any direct glare. She's awake, and I'm glad to see recognition in her eyes when she sees me.

"Hi, Dahlia. I missed you." I bend toward her, each movement slow enough to give her an opportunity to reject it and, when she doesn't, give her a gentle hug. She's been here but days, yet they haven't been kind to her frame. I need to discuss it further with Dr. Panakar, but she's lost at least ten pounds.

Dahlia doesn't return my embrace, but I don't hold it against her. I imagine every movement is hard right now. I scan the cast on her broken arm and notice familiar handwriting. Tears come to my eyes when I read "Ben" scrawled across the top. I force them away and point to his signature.

"Okay, who let Ben sign this first?" I put as much enthusiasm in my voice as I can and turn away to find a permanent marker of my own. On a nearby table, I find one, underneath cards left by Dahlia's friends in Shaconage and Maryville. Before I turn back toward

Dahlia, I paste a large smile on my face, one I hope she sees as genuine.

I take my time fussing over her cast, looking for the best spot to sign my name. With a flourish, I write my name...as far from Ben's as possible.

"Netta, why don't you sign it, too?" I hand her the marker and settle into the bed beside Dahlia, sure to avoid her broken leg, but snuggle in just the same. I take her good hand in mine.

Dahlia squeezes it gently, and we make eye contact. She's not talking yet, but her eyes say everything I need to hear. She's happy I'm home. She still loves me.

"I love you too." I smile at her, the first cheerful smile I've given in what feels like a lifetime, though I'm sure I've smiled even this week. I lie with her until she falls asleep, massaging her hand absently.

Being here with her soothes the ache a bit, even though it lingers around the edges. Netta loved the puzzle book, and as soon as I settled in with Dahlia, she retreated to the chair with a pen. Periodically, I catch her staring at me, but before I can speak, she returns to the page, scribbling away.

I leave her be, experience telling me she will speak her mind when she's ready. A nurse comes in to check Dahlia's vitals and offers to bring in some coffee. I'm bone weary, though I'm aware it's more emotional than physical. I accept the offer anyway and settle back into bed beside Dahlia with a steaming cup of black coffee.

With a huff, Netta closes her book and places it on the food table along with her pen. I sit up, ready for whatever she has to say. I place my cup on the table next to her puzzle book and rub my hands down my thighs.

"I've been watching you with Ben." Her words are blunt but without malice. I don't speak and, instead, wait for her to go on. "Ever since you got here, you've been fighting with that boy or practically cozied up. Just like when you were kids."

"I wouldn't say we've been cozy—"

She holds up her hand, cutting me off. "Let me finish, please." Leaning forward in her chair, she takes my hand in hers and holds my gaze. She looks at me for a couple of long moments before she breaks eye contact with a glance at Dahlia, who continues to sleep nearby.

"I haven't said much because you're a grown woman, and you can make your own choice about whom you spend your time with. I wouldn't say anything now if your young man from out west hadn't come by to visit Dahlia. Tate is his name, I believe."

"Wait, Tate came here?" Honestly, my mind is blown. I knew Tate cared about me but taking the time to visit Dahlia, a woman he's never met, was on an entirely different level.

"Yes, he came here and sat with Dahlia and me for a bit. He said he was headed home, that this was a quick visit." She gives me a long look. Unable to take the scrutiny, I break eye contact first, looking away and out the window. I sigh, and even I hear the agony in it.

"How do you choose between two good men?"

She pats my hand, and I take it in mine, holding on for dear life. "Nothing in this life is certain. When I met Harry, I had no idea that loving him would mean losing him. I've asked myself a hundred times over the years if I would have still married him, knowing I'd be a widow at such a young age. It's like Paul says in the Bible. Right now, we can only see what's in front of us, as if we are looking into a dim mirror. Soon, though, it will all make sense. At some point, you just have to take a step forward and let life happen, Cleo." Tears prick the corners of my eyes and I let out a shaky breath.

"These last few days with Ben have awakened a part of me that I thought was dead. On the other hand, Tate accepts me as I am; he's never tried to change me. And in the past, that's all Ben tried to do. It's all I ever tried to do." I frown down at our clasped hands.

"Since you've been back, has Ben tried to change you, to make you into someone else?"

"Hmm? No, I guess not. At first, he couldn't stand me being here, but as we've worked together, we've found a friendship, I guess. It's not the same as before." I take a deep breath and when I speak, the words tremble as they tumble out.

"It's better. It's...wonderful. He knows everything now. Why I left, why I married Vincent." Netta peers at me at the last but doesn't ask questions. She may be curious, but she's not one to pry.

"Well, I guess there's only one question to ask yourself at this point, Cleo." She squeezes my hand. "Who do you see yourself growing old with?"

It's not long before Netta leaves in search of lunch, and I'm left on my own. I take the seat recently vacated and consider our conversation. Growing old with someone is a huge commitment. You make promises to one another to stay, in the good times and the bad. Can I trust Ben to stick it out? He left me once already, in a different life and when we were practically kids. *But didn't he say he tried to come back?*

On the other hand, there's Tate. Dependable, lovable Tate. He'd never leave me; this I know for fact. If someone asked me whom I'd call my best friend, it would be him. We laugh, and we have so much in common. That should count for something, right?

Why, then, is it Ben I see when I close my eyes?

36

Relief fills me when I see Macy's familiar face peek around the door just after lunch. Netta has not yet returned from the cafeteria, and I've been ruminating on my own for far too long. We hug at the foot of Dahlia's bed and turn to study her together. I try to imagine what Dahlia looks like through Macy's eyes. This is the first time she's been allowed to visit her since Dahlia woke up. And before that, most people sent cards and flowers but didn't visit. I think most have given us space out of respect for Netta and me.

Dahlia is looking better, the bruises fading, though her broken limbs will take longer to heal. And once they are healed, she'll have a long journey in regaining the strength she's lost, lying in the bed for such an extended period. The physical therapy team here is incredible and they've been by to see Dahlia every day.

"She looks better than I imagined."

"Definitely better than when she first arrived, that's for sure." I walk around the bed and tuck her back in, making sure to smooth the hair that had fallen into her eyes. When she wakes up, I'll brush it. I make a mental note to bring in nail polish at the next visit. Dahlia has always prided herself on her appearance. Bright nail polish should elevate her mood.

"I haven't seen you in a couple of days." Macy picks at her nails. "I was surprised you stayed with Ben instead of with me."

I hear the hurt but ignore it. Instead, I steer the conversation toward her. "I feel like an ass, Macy. I still haven't met your guy."

She shrugs. "You will soon enough. There's forever, right?"

"Oh wow, this *is* serious. I mean, I saw the nursery, and you said you had plans, but I didn't realize things were falling into place so soon."

She sighs. "You've had a lot going on. I get it." Her posture says otherwise. "I mean, you have Dahlia and then there's Ben. Not to mention that other guy I saw you with at the diner." *Ah, there it is.* Jealousy.

I walk over to the window and hop up to sit on the ledge. When all this ends with Dahlia, I'm going to sit down with Macy and set some boundaries. She is my oldest friend, but she micromanages too much.

"That guy was Tate. My friend from home. He also manages my finances."

Her expression relaxes slightly before clamming up again. "What about Ben? Are you guys seeing each other now?"

"We're not." *I just slept with him last night.* That, I keep to myself. "It's a safety issue, Macy. We decided it was the best way to protect everyone involved."

Movement catches my eye, and I turn toward the bed in time to see Dahlia open her eyes. I smile and wait for her to recognize Macy. At first, she stares blankly at Macy. Worried, I push myself off the windowsill and start toward the bed, just as Macy takes her hand.

"Dahlia, it's Macy. Do you remember me?" Her tone is gentle as she speaks. At first, it's almost as if Dahlia doesn't see her at all. She stares straight ahead, unseeing. This proves to be short-lived.

Within seconds, all hell breaks loose. A blood-curdling scream erupts from Dahlia, and my heart seizes in fear. Despite her injuries, she nearly comes out of the bed swinging. Though it's hard to tell if it's at Macy or something unseen.

I dive toward the bed, half in and half out, and wrap my arms around Dahlia. "Dahlia, please, get back into bed. Please, lie down." Eyes wide, Macy backs away from the bed, her hands up in a defensive stance. Dahlia continues to scream, despite my efforts, and soon the hospital staff pours into the room.

I try to explain what happened as they help me get her back into bed.

No, she didn't seem to be in any pain before she started screaming.

No, we never left her alone.

Yes, I tried to calm her.

Yes, she seemed confused.

The questions continue, rapid-fire, as they take her from my arms and hold her down in the bed. All the while, Dahlia continues to scream, her voice pitching into a high-pitched wail I'll not soon forget. It's a sound that I'm certain will haunt my dreams.

A doctor enters, followed by a nurse with a syringe.

"Ms. Boucher, we're going to give you some medication to help you relax. You're very upset right now, and you're going to hurt yourself." With seemingly no awareness he'd spoken, she thrashes under the arms of the nurses. The doctor nods to the one with the syringe and within moments, Dahlia goes silent.

As if in sync, the room relaxes, and after a moment, a couple of the nurses step out. I walk over to Macy, who stands frozen by the door. I put my arm around her and turn to the doctor.

"What happened? She's been fine."

"It's hard to say. Her body and brain have been through significant trauma. Healing can take time." I tune him out when he starts talking about the science behind memory, my focus on Macy's pale face as she stares at Dahlia. For her part, Dahlia remains blissfully sedated.

When Netta returns, I quickly fill her in. Satisfied Dahlia is in good hands, I gently lead Macy from the room and to an empty chair outside.

37

If rest and relaxation were ever on the agenda for today, that idea is tossed completely out the window as soon as I get back to Ben's place. Anxious to avoid conversation, I scoop up the newspaper from the stoop and dart quickly up the stairs before going to my room and bolting the door.

I shower and change quickly, anxious to wash away as much of the day as possible. I pace around the bedroom as I consider my options. Option one: I stay here and pretend last night never happened. Two: I accept last night happened but put the brakes on it. Three: I can let things progress with Ben and see where they go. But if I choose that route, any future with Tate ends.

I flop onto the bed and pull the paper from its rubber band. Expecting to find a "Dear Abby" column or an article about the farmer's market, I flip the paper open with only the minimum amount of interest. To say I was shocked to find a photo of myself on the cover would be an understatement.

Front and center, a photo of me sitting with Macy on her front porch is flanked by a smaller photo of our friend group from high school. Off to the side, a small photo catches my eye, my hands tightening in an impossible grip on the paper. I take a deep breath and force myself to loosen my grip.

I read it all. Devin Mathews, the son-of-a-bitch, eavesdropped that night at Macy's, and he heard every-thing. His account is straightforward, and it is as detailed as an article in the local paper can be. Trevor's face mocks me from its place on the page. I stare at his face until he's a blur, tears pricking the corners of my eyes. With my vision blurred and ears ringing, I almost don't hear my phone as it starts to ping.

The first from Ben:

Can I come up?

I don't reply to that one.
The next one is from Alice, the florist.

Cleo, just read the paper. I'm sorry, hon.
Let me know if you need anything.

A panicked text from Macy is next.

I swear I didn't tell anyone. I don't know
how he found out.

I respond, reassuring her that I know exactly how he found out. It was my own damn fault, after all.

> He always seemed slimy.

That was from a waitress at Pop's.
Then, surprisingly, a text from Mariah DeMarco.

> Vince showed me the paper. We are here
> for you.

I type a response and delete several before placing the phone down next to me on the bed with a sigh.

I don't move when I hear Ben's steps on the stairs, when he knocks, or even when he opens the door with a key. I lie completely still, the paper scattered across the bed.

"Cleo." He eases into the room, his eyes on the newspaper. "Talk to me, sweetheart." He pauses when he reaches me and then slowly leans down to press a kiss on my forehead. That's all it takes for me to start crying.

Though no longer visible, the newspaper continues to haunt me. Once a secret pain only I knew, Trevor's abuse would never be secret again. Part of me is relieved, another part is terrified Trevor will find out. Fear grips me, my body going rigid in Ben's arms.

He's lying next to me on the bed, holding me close, lips murmuring sweet and comforting things into my hair. Half of them, I can't hear, but it's pleasant and soothes the ache in my chest. Just a bit.

He runs his hand up and down my arm, and I feel my

body relax slightly against him. This doesn't mean we're together. This is a friend comforting a friend. Tomorrow. Tomorrow, I'll tell him we can't be more than that. Today, well, today I need his arms around me.

Insistent ringing jerks me from sleep, but for once, it's not my phone. The sky has melted into blackness while we slept, and I reach blindly toward the bedside table and turn on the lamp. When the light flicks on, I see Ben has sat up and retrieved his phone from where he discarded it when he came in earlier.

"DeMarco." All business, his tone is curt, and I can't help the small trill of excitement it gives me. How is he even hotter when he's on the job? Those butterflies evaporate when he turns to me.

"It's Macy. She's hurt." I'm halfway out the door when his hand encircles my arm, stopping me in my tracks.

"Wait. I'll take you." He releases his hold on me when I hesitate.

"I can take myself, Ben. I don't need you to coddle me." My arms cross at my chest.

"You won't be able to see her without me. Until I have her statement, there's a guard on her door at the hospital."

My arms drop to my sides in shock, and I can't help the gasp that strangles out of me.

"Hospital? Oh, God. How bad is she hurt?" My mind

has gone to the worst—to Dahlia. Oh, please. Don't let it be like that.

"She'll be fine, Cleo. She's pretty banged up, but she'll be fine."

I don't bother responding; instead, I walk back into the bedroom to retrieve my keys and phone. Ben doesn't move from his spot in the living room where I hear him barking orders into the phone. When I come back out, he ends the call.

"Let's go." I don't make eye contact as we exit. If my stalker is unafraid to go after those I care about, what's stopping him from going after Ben? Ben will be safer if the stalker thinks I hate him.

I repeat this to myself on the drive to the hospital and do my best to avoid conversation with him on the way. Once we arrive, I keep my distance, even as we walk into the hospital together. It's for the best.

38

As soon as we're spotted, we're directed to a private room in the emergency department. It's windowless and empty except for an examination table and two chairs. When we open the door, the two uniformed officers inside leave us alone with Macy.

Dried blood is crusted around her nose, her left eye black. Scratch marks are gouged into her jaw, and it's clear that whoever attacked her meant business. I walk forward and give her a gentle hug before stepping out of the way. I notice a bruise has started to form on her neck. She's been choked. Fury rises in me and threatens to spill over, but I force myself to take deep breaths, to keep my mouth shut. The last thing I want is to be tossed out for interfering. Instead, I listen, making mental notes of everything.

"When did this happen?" Ben asks as he sets a tape recorder on the table.

"I'd been out, and when I got home, the porch light was out. I thought nothing of it since I can't remember the last time I switched it out for a new one. Anyway, it was dark, so I didn't see him standing on the porch when I first came up." She pauses to take a deep breath. "It was Mark Jeffers."

A breath I was holding whooshes out of me at the words.

Ben doesn't react at all. "You're sure it was him?"

"Yes, I'm sure. Who in town doesn't know who Jeffers is, especially after the accident?" She gestures toward me as she speaks, and I nod. Jeffers and his wife were from the area but not Shaconage. If not for the accident highlighting them, he might have been unknown to Macy and others here. Vincent's death made him notorious.

"All right. What happened once you came onto the porch and saw Mr. Jeffers?"

"He didn't say much. I was shocked to see him there and kind of froze a bit." She looks at me and fidgets in a way I can only interpret as anxious. Reliving this must be hell.

"He mentioned Cleo. I think he was drunk; no, he was definitely drunk. His breath was horrible, smelled like Bud Light." She shudders and continues, "He said it was all Cleo's fault, and I got scared. I tried to run away. That's when he grabbed me. He started choking me and threw me on the ground. It was awful."

Ben continues to ask her questions, asking her to elaborate on detail after detail. I sit in the corner and try to remain neutral. Macy needs me to remain calm right now. I can do that for both of us. Now, at least, I know my enemy.

My phone vibrates in my hand, and I glance toward the others to see if it was noticed. They continue with their interview, unaware. I tap the screen to see a message from an unknown number.

Curious, I open it and scan it quickly, panic knotting my gut.

> YOU FUCKING BITCH. How dare you spread lies around town about me when you know anything we shared was consensual? I can't believe you. My mother is near dying of shame over your shit. Imagine me needing to force white trash like you to have sex with me. It's laughable. Maybe you need a reminder of how good we are together. Is that what this is? Some pathetic attempt to get my attention? Well, you've got it. You won't forget this time.

> See you soon.

The last thing I expected was to open my phone to a text from Trevor. A chill rolls through me at the thought of his hands on me. I won't go through that again. I refuse to allow him to make me his victim. I take a screenshot of the message and send it to Ben. His phone pings, but I don't look at him and Macy. Their conversation continues, but I don't hear it. I send the same message to Tate.

I know we have a lot to talk about and I'm not asking you to pretend everything is okay. I know it's not. But I've got a problem here. An article was published about my sexual assault. Trevor knows. I forwarded you the text. Can you please have your guy keep tabs on him? xx

After I hit send, I pull up the text conversation with Trevor and block the number. Then I go on every social media account registered to my business and block every single one of his personal accounts. I hope it's enough.

It's not long before Ben wraps up the interview, and Macy agrees to stay overnight for observation. I stay with her until she's settled and make her promise to call me if she needs me. I make the short trip upstairs and check in on Dahlia and extract a promise from Netta that she'll go home for some rest tomorrow.

Ben is waiting for me by the truck when I come out, but says nothing until we're inside and buckled. He turns toward me in the seat, the leather squeaking with the movement.

"I got your text. Have you had any other contact with Trevor since the assault?"

I start to remind him about the rose, but he beats me to it, cutting me off. "Other than the one rose he sent on the first anniversary."

I shake my head and sigh.

"I do wonder if he's sent any others over the years. Something tells me Dahlia would have kept it to herself. I never told her what he did, but I think she must have suspected. I was a mess when I received it back then."

I close my eyes and rest my head on the back of the seat. When will this end? If it's not one thing, it's another. Coming back here was dangerous. I should have asked Dahlia to move to Arizona years ago. As soon as I think it, I discard it. Truthfully, I know she never would have left this place, not after ninety-plus years here.

Without opening my eyes, I ask him about Jeffers. "Have they found Jeffers yet? It would be so nice to be able to sleep at Dahlia's house again." I say it casually, reminding myself that Ben needs to think I'm unaffected by the recent sex we've had.

"We haven't located him yet. You're stuck with me for at least one more night." His tone is calm enough as he speaks. My heart jumps, despite my best efforts to remain detached.

When we pull up outside the apartment, neither of us speaks or even looks at the other. I grab my bag from the floor and follow him slowly up the stairs. I walk to my room and toss my bag on the chair in the corner. Closing my eyes, I take a deep breath before walking back to the door, which had swung partially shut behind me as I came in. I place my hand on it to shut it, but pause when I see him just outside.

Ben is standing still in the middle of the living room, his eyes on me. When we make eye contact, his gaze sets me ablaze, and my bruised heart flutters. Without a single word, I pull the door fully open and step back. A silent invitation.

He takes it.

39

The panic I felt yesterday morning is absent when I wake today. This time, I snuggle in closer to Ben and let myself breathe him in. Whether or not this can go anywhere is not important right now. Still asleep, he pulls me closer, enveloping me in his arms. For the first time since I got here, I feel safe.

Too soon, the alarm sounds, and he awakens. He smiles through sleepy eyes, and my heart turns over in my chest. It's the kind of smile that you fall into, that keeps you coming back. I give him a small one in return, and it's enough to have him hitting snooze. He reaches for me and I laugh as he kisses my lips.

Later, I make breakfast and check my emails, relieved to have a name for my stalker. Ben and his men continue to look for him, but I'm not worried. I'm safely tucked away in an apartment above the sheriff's station—I'm in the safest place possible at this point.

I scroll through texts, finding several messages asking after Macy, which I respond to first. Others from friends back in Arizona, which admittedly, I have thought little of since I got here. I ignore those. There will be plenty of time for catching up…after.

Tate responds just as I expected. I can tell from the wording of his messages that he is trying to be respectful of my space and feelings. That man is far too good for me. Maybe that's the problem. Ben and I are both seriously fucked up. How could we not be after all we've been through? But not Tate. I don't want to taint him with it.

I read his texts, starting at the top and growing increasingly alarmed with each one.

> Of course, Cleo. I will contact him today and request he give me a quick update on Trevor's whereabouts.

Then,

> My guy has lost contact with him. He's tracking him and will update us soon.

Finally,

> He's at home in Atlanta. I'll ask my guy to trail him.

The last message came in early this morning, around five a.m. It's after two now. There have been no updates since then. I hit dial and wait to hear his voice, but he doesn't answer. Frowning, I lower the phone and hit end call. Tate always answers. Could it be that he's done waiting for me? But isn't that what I wanted? This morning, lying in Ben's arms, I had almost decided it was. What if there are no more calls, no more texts between us?

That's when I feel it—every piece of me coming unraveled, falling in a puddle at my feet. There's nothing left to do but try my best to pick up the strings of my snarled, knotted, and destroyed heart.

On my way out, I stop by the station to ask for transport to Dahlia's house. I need more clothing, and honestly, I'd like to get my paints. If I'm going to be at Ben's for the foreseeable future, I need my things.

I barrel through the door, nearly smacking into Deputy Franks. He huffs and murmurs something about "kids" under his breath as he leaves. I make eye contact with Leah behind the desk, and we both laugh.

"Is Sheriff DeMarco here?" I keep my tone as professional as possible and hope the heat I feel isn't obvious.

"Actually—" She stops speaking when the door behind me opens, and I hear Ben's voice. I whirl to see him walking Mark Jeffers in, cuffed. He doesn't see me at first, focused on his task. Jeffers, on the other hand, misses nothing. As soon as his feet hit the threshold, he starts cussing me.

"You bitch. You ruined my life once; you think you

can do it again?" He jerks in Ben's hold, which tightens when he sees me standing in the room.

"Cleo, can you wait in my office, please?"

He continues past me, dragging a struggling Jeffers, who seems balanced despite his drunkenness and ill-fitting prosthetic. He doesn't look my way again, so I turn back to the receptionist, following her toward the back. She leaves me in Ben's office, which is smaller than I expected.

He takes longer than I expected, so I take a seat behind his desk and study the items there. The top of his desk has little on it—a pen, a few papers, a folder. A nameplate and cup holder completes the look. I spin in his chair, taking in the room as I do. I stop when I see a bookshelf with a few photos scattered between the books.

With a glance at the door, I approach the shelf to study them, one by one. The first is a photo of Ben and Vincent as children. Another photo of his parents at some holiday party. The last photo takes my breath away. I pull the photo from the shelf and study it for too long.

The door opens, then clicks quietly as it closes. Slow footsteps cross the room to stop just behind me. I take a deep breath before I turn and hold the photo out to him.

"It's me." Wonder seeps into my voice. I can't help it. "You have a photo of me. Here?"

He stares down at it for a long moment before putting it back on the shelf. Instead of speaking, he leans down and places a sweet kiss on my mouth. He straightens and holds my gaze for a moment before walking around the desk and taking a seat.

For a moment, I don't move. My mind is fuzzy, and I'm confused. How long has the photo been there? All this time? Knees weak, I take three steps forward and sit in the closest chair.

Ben clears his throat, forcing my gaze to focus on his face, on his words.

"Jeffers denies attacking Macy. At this point, it's he said, she said." A protest forms on my lips, but he holds up a hand, quieting me. "Of course, he's also made threats to you, and we're taking prints and waiting on DNA results. He won't get away with it, Cleo." His gaze is kind when he speaks to me.

I nod and sniff, realizing I'm on the verge of a breakdown. I stand up quickly and brush my hands down my pants. Now that it's all over, I'm nervous and anxious to be alone with him here.

Shakily, I talk as I walk toward the door, "Well, then. I, uh, I'll pack up my stuff and head back to Dahlia's. I really appreciate everything you've done—" The rest is lost as I find myself crushed against him, his mouth claiming mine, so forceful it hurts.

"You're not leaving."

Questions swirl, but I don't voice them. Does he mean he doesn't want me to leave tonight or ever? I'm afraid to know the answer. His mouth takes mine again, gentle this time, as he runs his fingers through my long hair. He bites my lip, and I'm lucky I don't disintegrate on the spot. My arms tighten around him, if only to hold myself up.

A knock on the door has us moving apart, though he moves slowly, as if reluctant to let go. Almost as if he's not worried about being seen touching me. I file that away for later. Deputy Franks enters and hands him a folder, which he thumbs through.

"I'll see you later?"

He nods, never taking his eyes off the papers in front of him. With a sigh of relief, I make my exit.

Well aware of the cowardice I'm exhibiting, I make quick work of packing my things, dumping them into the Rogue before going home to Dahlia's place. Ben has made it clear he'd like me to stay at his place, but to what end? If I continue down this road with him, where will I end up? Will it last, or will I find myself alone, grieving the loss of him yet again?

Dahlia's place comes into view quickly, and I park in front, pulling my bag out of the back and dragging it across the lawn. The chickens are out of the pen, and I make a note to fix it before bedtime. Dahlia will have my hide if I let a fox get ahold of her chickens.

The house looks tidy, and it occurs to me that Ben must have had someone in to clean it up after the techs were through with it. My feelings for that man are a rollercoaster. When I walk into my childhood bedroom, it feels cold. Now that I've had a couple of days with Ben, sleeping alone is the last thing I want.

I throw the suitcase on the bed and unfold it, busying

myself with unpacking instead of allowing myself to dwell on thoughts of "what-ifs" with Ben. When I'm done, I push the case into the corner of the room. I search for my cell phone before remembering I left it in the car.

I find it in the cup holder, but it's dead when I retrieve it. *Great.* I press the power button a couple of times, but it's useless. It's definitely dead. I fish the cell-phone charger out of the console and shove it into my pocket before turning back toward the house.

I almost stumble when I see him standing on the porch steps, a sick smirk stretching his face wide.

Trevor.

41

" **I** told you I'd see you soon." He swaggers toward me, confident and sure. With every step he advances, I retreat. At first, he seems amused by it. Quickly, though, he becomes impatient with the game, and familiar darkness creeps into his eyes. He increases his pace, anger radiating from him.

I turn and run toward the back of the house, to the barn. When I hear him gaining on me, I push my legs harder. I ran track in school, and I'm a frequent runner now. Despite this, he catches up to me before I reach the door and yanks me back by my long ponytail.

"Where are you going, Cleo? We're supposed to be catching up." His tone is calm but the kind that makes your skin crawl. His posture is combative. I hit his fist with mine, trying to pry his hands from my hair, without success. He laughs, delighting in my struggle.

"There's the Cleo I know and love." He pulls me close and turns me toward him. With horror, I realize he intends to kiss me.

"NO." My voice rings across the yard, strong and commanding. This is not happening again. It will *never* happen again.

"Yes," he tells me as he closes the distance between us with each twist of my hair, reeling me in like a fish on a hook. I let my body go slack, feigning acquiescence. Just as I feel his grip loosen on my hair, I slam my head hard into his nose.

Head ringing, I stumble back from him, my vision blurring as I try my best to flee. Near me, just out of sight, I hear him screaming that I'd broken his nose. I ignore him and continue to stagger away from his voice.

As my vision clears, I see him straighten himself, his hand dropping from his face to let the blood flow freely. I'm scared. No one knows I'm here. The phone in my pocket is dead. If I can't get away, he can do whatever he wants to me, and no one will ever know. My steps seesaw as I do my best to run toward the back of the house; my head screaming at me, warning me that I need to lie down and rest.

Fear pushes me forward, and I make it up the steps and to the back door, only slightly swaying with each step. Just as my hand clasps the knob, he catches me, pulling me against him, his hands going to my throat. Tighter and tighter, he squeezes as he pushes me toward Dahlia's favorite wicker couch. I punch at his hands without success.

He shoves me onto the couch. The force of it has the couch coming off the ground to slam into the railing before hitting the floor again. I gasp for breath, my hand at my throat. He could kill me so easily. He knows it, and now I do too. I tremble. He watches me with satisfaction, licking his bloody lips. For the first time since I laid eyes on him, I see the end. They'll never find my body.

I open my mouth to curse or to beg, I'm not sure, but my words are cut short when he slaps me hard across the face. The sting has the opposite effect than the one he wanted. Instead of silencing me, making me weak, it fans the flame. *I'm not a victim. If I'm dying today, I won't make it easy for him.*

I kick out at him, catching him in the knee. He grunts at the impact but doesn't move away. Despite my flailing body, he manages to crawl on top of me, holding me down. He grabs my face, kissing me hard, biting the corner of my lip and drawing blood. He spits the blood into my face. "You deserved that. Be a good girl now."

Despite my best efforts, I can't move. He has my arms pinned on the couch next to my hips. I'm effectively paralyzed and at his mercy. He shifts on top of me, pushing my left hand up and closer to my hip. That's when I feel it. The cellphone charging cord.

Hope blooms in me, and I give him a meek nod. A nod that says I'll do anything so long as he doesn't hurt me. I do my best to relax underneath him, and just as I hoped, he relaxes too, my pathetic state giving him an overabundance of confidence.

Assured of my cooperation, he releases my arms to slide his hands under my crop top to grope my breasts. I let him do it just long enough to ensure he's relaxed before I strike. Distracted, he doesn't see my hand move before it's too late. I reach between us and grab his penis and twist it as hard as I can. He recoils with a screech so loud, I'm sure all of Shaconage heard it.

The brief disconnection of his body from mine gives me the space I need to pull the cord from my pocket. Focus elsewhere, he doesn't see it coming. I slip the cord around his throat, crossing it behind his neck, and squeeze it with every ounce of strength I have.

At first, he claws at it, but after a moment, he switches to punching me in the head. I do my best to tuck my face but continue to tighten the orange cord, looping it over and over in my hands, making it tighter and tighter.

Ben and Deputy Franks find us like this. It takes some time, but Ben pries the cord from my fingers, the pressure having cut into the palms. It takes even longer for me to stop screaming and it isn't until I stop that I realize I was. An ambulance arrives at some point, and Deputy Franks leaves with what's left of Trevor. Sadly, it seems, despite my best efforts, he'll live.

For a while, I sit in silence on that wicker couch. My mind is completely blank. I feel cold, even though I know it's eighty-five degrees out today. That must be the shock. There's a loud buzz in my ears, blocking out the activity around me. Occasionally, I hear Ben's voice break through, but I couldn't tell you a word of what he said. Eventually, I don't hear anything at all.

Harsh light wakes me, a headache forming the moment I open my eyes. I try to use my hands to push up, to sit. Pain rips through me with every movement I try to make. My groan wakes Ben from his spot near the door.

"Cleo, lie down." He tries to coax me back down, but I smack at his hand.

"Don't make me lie down." My voice is raspy in my throat. "Please." Every word is torture, but I need him to understand me. I need to sit up.

Tears pool in the corners of his eyes, and his hands clench into fists at his sides. He takes a step back and gives me space to breathe.

"I need a mirror." He hesitates before walking to the sink and retrieving a small medical mirror. He hands it to me, though he doesn't let of go it.

"It's okay," I tell him. "It's okay." When he drops his hand, I raise the mirror to my face and stare at my reflection, careful to avoid showing any reaction to what I see there. A bruise feathers across my temple and around my neck. I touch my hair, remembering how hard he pulled it. When I pull my hand away, a fistful of hair comes with it. I frown at it. Ben steps toward me with a plastic bag. Without a word, I put the hairs inside and watch him seal it.

Eyes on the mirror once more, I focus in on my split lip. I reach up and touch it, wincing as the movement irritates the cuts on my palms. Flecks of dried blood spot my face, making me ill. Forcing myself to stand, the action sends me tilting to the side as I do so. I rush to the sink and vomit.

Before I can wash my face, Ben stops me. *Right. My*

body is evidence now. The next few hours are a blur of photos, specimens, and, despite my protests that it was unnecessary, a pelvic exam.

I don't fight Ben when he takes me back to his place. Instead of depositing me in the guest room, he carries me up the stairs and into his room. Gently, he lays me on his bed and removes the hospital socks from my feet. He retrieves an old T-shirt from his dresser, returning to the bed to undress me. He pulls the paper scrubs from my sore body and replaces them with his shirt.

He takes care of me; his movements are soft and careful. After he finishes, he stands to leave, but I grab his hand, stopping him. He looks down at me with questions in his eyes.

"How did you know where I was?"

"Your friend Tate called. His P.I. tracked Trevor to Shaconage. He couldn't reach you, so he called the station and asked for me. When I realized you left, Franks and I left immediately." He closes his eyes for a moment and expels a shaky breath. "When I think of what could have happened... I—" He shakes his head before whispering, "I can't lose you too."

"I'm okay, Ben." The pain coursing through my body says otherwise, and I grimace at the white lie. Ben needs the truth from me, now more than ever. "All right, I'm not okay, but I will be. *I will be.*" I squeeze his hand, and he squeezes it back, careful of the bandages there. He turns back to me and begins to lower himself to sit.

A knock sounds downstairs, jerking Ben back to his feet. He leaves to see who's at the door, and I busy myself with arranging the blankets around me. Muffled voices turn to heated words as the voices grow closer to the room.

"She needs to rest." I hear Ben's voice over the others, his tone expecting no argument. The door swings open anyway, and I find myself face-to-face with my mother-in-law. Nervous about being found in Ben's bed, I try to sit up, the motion painful. I wince, grabbing my side. Before I can attempt any other movement, Mariah is at my side, her hands pushing me back into the covers.

"Cleo, don't move. You need to rest." I'm shocked at the tears in her eyes. Tears for *me*. She fusses with the duvet, telling Ben to adjust the thermostat, so I won't be cold.

"Mariah, it's fine. You don't need to do this."

"Yes, I do!" Her voice is shrill, but not from anger. She looks like she's trying not to cry. I reach out to her to try to comfort her in some way. But when she sees the bandage on my hand, she sobs. I drop my hand, letting it rest on the bed.

Panicked, I look at Ben, who wears an expression identical to mine. Frozen, he doesn't move, only stares at his mother. Mariah continues to cry and adjust my pillows, the blankets, anything but look at me.

"Mariah, I'm okay. You don't need to worry about me."

"Cleo, yes I *do*." Her voice drops, and I can see the fervor in her eyes as she speaks. "I do need to worry about you, Cleo. You're my family. No matter the past, you're important to us. I'm sorry I pushed you away. I thought you were going to hurt both of my sons, and it made me angry. I'm sorry for it all."

I shake my head, somehow anxious to relieve her pain.

"No, don't minimize it. I hurt you—we—hurt you. As a family and as a community. Bennett and Vincent Jr. made their choices. We were wrong." Her voice raises in volume as she continues, "And when I saw that photo of what happened to you today, I was furious. The nerve of that man, coming after *my* family. When we're done with him, he'll wish he never crossed the DeMarco family."

She continues to rant, but I don't hear the rest. There was another photo. *God.* Does Devin Mathews follow me everywhere? I see Ben take his phone from his pocket and do a quick search. After a moment, he frowns at me and nods.

A single tear escapes, making tracks down my face. The reality of today's trauma hits me like a ton of bricks. Ben, somehow so in tune with me, sees the change. He ushers Mariah out with a promise that she can visit again tomorrow.

Within moments, he returns to the room and crawls into the bed next to me. I let the tears fall until they dry up, but he doesn't seem to mind. He simply holds me and gives me the safety of his arms.

42

What would I have done without Ben beside me when I got the news that Dahlia had passed in the night? Initially, the grief I expected was missing. Later, I was able to attribute my apathy to the painkillers.

The news caught everyone off guard, even her doctors. At the time of her death, her prognosis for a full recovery had been good—a long road but good. After, everyone agreed her age simply caught up with her.

The worst part was that for the last two days of her life, I wasn't able to be with her. I was at Ben's, doing my best to heal from Trevor's assault. I asked Ben if Dahlia's death would be attributed to Jeffers' attack, but even he wasn't sure. We are waiting for the official report from the medical examiner before further action can be determined.

When I meet with Dahlia's attorney, I learn she left me almost everything—all the way down to the chickens. She took care of Netta too. Unsurprisingly, Dahlia opted to be cremated, just as her family had for generations.

Netta helps me plan and execute a beautiful memorial service to honor Dahlia and the legacy she left behind. So many people—far more than just I—owed their success to her. She embodied the image of a caring, Christian woman…something so rarely seen these days.

The church is packed for the service, with many people lined up out the door and around the corner. The minister opens the windows so those waiting outside can hear. Dahlia, who loved being loved, would be pleased with the turnout.

Throughout these days, I am alone a lot, resting under a cloud of oxycodone. Ben and Mariah—and even Vince—are with me as much as they can be, but they have priorities outside of me. Netta—bless her heart—spends her time going through Dahlia's things, donating what she can to those in need.

It's over now. My sweet grandmother's ashes are on their way to be packaged and stored in an urn. I'm truly alone now. I don't know if I'll ever be okay again. I knew eventually the day would come that I'd be the last of my family—even my child gone before me—but I was not prepared for the depth of pain I'd feel when it happened.

43

Ben smiles so bright when he sees me, I wince. His affection and care have been achingly beautiful these last few days. Since I lost Dahlia, he's been loving, giving me space and, alternately, closeness as my mood has fluctuated. Once I no longer relied on the pain medication, he let me grieve Dahlia anew and fully. He never left my side.

Regardless, I've continued to mistrust him. Maybe the past is too big to ignore. He might always leave. I can't help but think back to that conversation with Netta. Who, exactly, do I see myself growing old with?

From across the room, he motions for me to meet him in his office, so I give a short wave to Leah and let myself in. I walk over to the bookcase and pick up the photo of me. It's an old one, taken not long before the pregnancy—before Ben left. We were on a hike when he snapped it. I'm still holding it when he comes in.

"I love that photo. It was the last one we took together."

"I had forgotten about that day." I place the frame back on the shelf. I pace in the small the space. Unbothered, Ben leans against the door and watches me, waits for me to speak first.

The seconds stretch into minutes until, finally, I come to a stop, far away from him on the other side of the room. For this, I need my space. I've worked myself up so much that I feel my heart racing, threatening to beat right out of my chest. I remind myself to breathe.

"I'm leaving."

His relaxed posture evaporates, my unexpected words jolting him. He straightens and stares at me, his jaw clenched. He doesn't speak, even though his eyes tell me he wants to.

"I'm going back to Arizona. I have a life there. A career." Building up steam, I resume my pacing as I continue. "All of my friends are in Arizona, and frankly, I prefer the weather." I wince at that. *I prefer the weather? Come on, Cleo. You can do better than that.*

"I'm sure you didn't know this, but I'm pretty involved in a women's program there—it's important to me. I sponsor women leaving domestic violence relationships. We've helped a lot of women in the last few years. They need me."

He clears his throat. "I didn't know that." He no longer appears defensive, more reluctant now.

"Yeah, and I need to get back to them. Plus, I have so many projects to wrap up, and then there's my house..." I'm rambling now. I know it, and I think he does too.

"But, Cleo, you can do all of those things from here." He pauses for a moment, then adds, "If you want to."

"Are you...Are you asking me to stay?" This is it. Either he wants me, or he doesn't.

"I can't make that decision for you."

Oh. I thought he was making a declaration of love, but I was wrong. I nod and can't help the small sniff as my eyes tear up. Once again, he doesn't want me. Heartbreak greets me like an old friend, and I grasp ahold of it like a lifeline.

"Why would I stay here, right? Everything I have is in Arizona. My whole life." It's best to make a clean break, so I take a deep breath and end it for good. "Tate is waiting for me, and I think he could be the one."

The lie sits heavy on my tongue, its acid making me sick with self-hate. Even if I go back now, I know there's no future with Tate. These last weeks with Ben have shown me where my heart belongs. But Ben doesn't know that. He can't know that, not now.

Ben walks over to me, though not angry, as he generally is when I mention Tate. The only word I can think of to describe him right now is resigned. My heart turns to ash when he leans down to give me a soft kiss before leaving me alone in the room.

It was stupid of me to wish he'd fight for me. But, once again, he's fine with parting. Anger fuels me, and I quickly gather my things from his apartment and make my way to Dahlia's—*my*—house. I hate that. I hate that it's my house. I let myself cry it out on the drive over. Why the hell not? If I want to cry, I think I've earned it at this point.

I pull into the driveway and sit for a moment, taking it in. I'll need to do something about the house at some point. Guilt washes over me when I think about selling. Without Dahlia here—and this recent, raw episode with Bennett—I don't think I can hold on to it. I don't think I'll ever come back. The chickens, on the other hand...I hope they like Arizona because I can't desert them. For now, I'll ask Netta to take care of them.

I pull out my phone and send a quick text to Macy.

> Hey, Mace. I'm headed back to Phoenix. I'm packing now. I'll be back in a few weeks to close the house.

She responds immediately.

> Really, Cleo? You have to stop running away when things get hard. Is this because of Ben? You have more here than just him. What about me?

Dahlia is gone. I have Netta, of course, and Macy, but it's not enough to uproot my life. It's just not enough.

> I'm sorry. I need to go. We'll talk soon, I promise.

It's shitty of me, but it's the best I can do. Staying here is not an option, especially not after the scene at the station. I can't face Ben again. I grab my suitcase and satchel from the back and trudge up the steps, each step heavy. Damn Ben and this whole town for making this harder than it needs to be. Like a mantra, I tell myself over and over that it's for the best. And it is. *It is.*

44

There's not much to pack. A few paintings I did while here, my suitcase of art supplies, athletic wear, and my computer sum up my short-lived existence here. I take my time going from room to room, savoring the lingering smell of Dahlia's perfume. It won't last, eventually fading from her sweaters and leaving the house altogether. Soon, it will exist only in my memory.

I sit on her bed, stroking the patchwork quilt. Dahlia made this when I was a child. A memory comes to me easily, of a much younger Cleo sitting next to her at the dining room table while she pinned the pieces together. Standing up, I pull the blanket from the bed and carefully fold it. I hear my phone ringing and exit Dahlia's room, closing the door gently behind me. When I reach my room, the ringing has stopped. I leave the phone on the bed, the red light flashing.

The quilt just fits into the cramped space of my suitcase and, satisfied I've packed everything I need, zip it and close it. My phone pings, signaling an incoming message. Ben's name fills the screen. I key in my passcode and open his message.

Devin is dead.

I don't get the chance to respond. A floorboard behind me groans under the pressure of another person's weight and then—darkness.

45

Panic greets me like an old friend when I come to, only to find myself in darkness. I'm lying flat on what feels like a bed and moving proves difficult. Pain zings through my head with every motion. I'm sure this is due to the knock to the head I took back at Dahlia's place. I touch the back of my head now, relief filling me to find no blood on my fingers when I pull them away. At least that's one problem I don't have.

As the night passes into morning, light begins to filter through the tiny window on the opposite side from where I'm lying. As the light grows and expands, I see that I'm in a basement. That explains the musty smell.

By this point, the ringing has melted into a dull ache. Braver now, I sit up, wincing when sharpness echoes through my head. Okay, so not totally better. I close my eyes and focus on taking a slow breath, allowing the sensation to pass.

When I open my eyes and take in the room for the

first time, I'm tempted to close them again. The basement is small and unfinished, though I'm grateful to find that it is at least floored in cement. But what sends chills down my spine are the hundreds of photos on the walls as well as the sight of my missing paintings, even some that must have been purchased from my website. My work is everywhere here.

Covering every inch of the walls are pieces of me. Snapshots of me in Shaconage, in Arizona, and even on trips to Paris and Seattle. It seems that everywhere I've gone in the last decade is documented on these walls.

Articles about my work are tacked between photos of me shopping, sleeping, and laughing. Ticket stubs to my shows are taped to some photos, and I recognize some of them, remember some of those nights.

Bile rises in my throat when I see a photo of Ben and me, naked and lost in one another at his place, in his bed. This one is recent, mere days ago. I turn in a circle, studying them one by one. A photo catches my eye, one of me on my wedding day that wasn't in the papers. Grainy and dark, it's difficult to see from my spot by the bed.

I step forward to see it better, but I'm stopped short, my ankle wrenched. Sharp pain pulls my attention away from the photo. "No. No. No," I chant the word when I see my ankle shackled to the bed, a short chain me holding me in place. But it's not the shackle that has me falling to my knees. It's the white wedding gown I'm wearing, a dress nearly identical to one I've worn before.

When the door to the basement opens and footsteps start down the steps, I don't bother to look up. Seated on the floor, pieces of the dress in tatters around me, I flinch when my captor reaches me. "What a waste of Chanel. Honestly, Cleo."

Fingers wrap around my chin, cupping it in a hard grip. I try to jerk away, but I'm forced to look up and into the eyes of my best friend.

For her part, Macy appears amused. Her eyes take me in, trailing across my face and down my gown, pausing at my feet, drops of red dotting the hem. With a small frown, she pulls the gown away from my legs to peer down at my raw and bloody ankle. "Jesus, Cleo. You're going to hurt yourself."

Her tone is equal parts tender and parental. It makes me sick. "What is going on, Macy?" Why would she do this? It doesn't make sense.

"You were going to leave. I couldn't go through that again. I need you, Cleo." She runs her long fingers across my cheek, and I flinch, pulling away. She doesn't push the issue but stands and walks over to the photo wall, running her fingers across a photo of me from last year at the beach.

"After everything I've done for you, I thought you'd be more grateful. Sometimes, I feel like I'm the only person in this relationship."

"What do you mean, after all you've done?"

"For starters, I took care of Devin for you. He'll never

sneak around taking photos of you again. I mean, honestly, don't we deserve a little privacy after everything?"

She smiles at me and picks up a bottle of water, opening it and it extending it to me. I take it as she continues.

"I called him up and told him you were ready to do an interview but on your terms. He came easily enough. Unfortunately, things got a little...messy. He put up a good fight and managed to get a couple of good hits in." She winces as she rubs her neck, my mom's locket securely fastened around it. Then, abruptly, she laughs.

"It was so easy to pin it on Mark Jeffers. Everyone knows he has a grudge against you, and more than one person has seen him at Dahlia's in the past. I merely used it to my benefit." She shrugs and runs her fingers through her short hair.

I clear my throat, looking for the right words. "But why do it at all? You could have just come to me with your feelings. You didn't have to—oh my god. *You* hurt Dahlia?" It's unbelievable. Dahlia loved Macy almost as much as she loved me. "You sent the letters?"

"Seriously, Cleo. Catch up. I must have hit you on the head harder than I thought. Sorry about that, by the way, but I had to be sure you'd come here." Here in the basement, chained and helpless, her smile seems to grow more malicious by the minute.

I crawl toward the bed, putting as much distance between us as possible. If she sent the letters, hurt Dahlia, it's clear there are no limits to her insanity. That must be why Dahlia freaked out when she woke up. She *knew* it was Macy. "Dahlia remembered you. She knew it was you."

She nods, her smile plastic and large. "I guess it's *convenient* she passed in her sleep." Her laugh stops me, and that's when the truth hits me. "You killed her."

This time I don't meet her eyes. If I do, she'll see how much I despise her. Something tells me I need to play along. I smooth my hands down my legs and will myself to calm.

"Wow. That's a lot, Macy. I can't believe you did all that for me." She moves closer, and I do my best not to cringe when her fingers caress my hair. She leans down and presses a kiss to the top of my head.

"I've done more." She whispers it against me before dropping to sit beside me.

I force myself to make eye contact, will my face to stay neutral and inviting.

"Cleo, I've been trying to get you to see me for years. I've always been here. I was here before Bennett, and I would have been here after if you had let me." She frowns at me, and I suck in a breath, suddenly frightened of this girl I've known my whole life. She springs to her feet and walks over to the wall, ripping a photo from it before coming back to fling it in my face.

"But no, as soon as Ben was out of the picture, you had to go and get with his brother. You betrayed me, Cleo. You betrayed us. So I did what I had to do. I wasn't going to let you and Vincent freaking DeMarco live a white-picket life while I pined away in the corner."

I stare at the grainy photo of Vincent's cold body cradled in my arms and feel tears prick my eyes. "What did you do?" I whisper it, half-hoping she won't hear me. She does.

"You have to understand my position, Cleo. You left me for him. I was angry." Her tone is pleading, like a lover who's fucked up. She reaches out to me, and I don't hide my disgust this time. "What. Did. You. Do." The words hiss out between my teeth, each one more venomous than the last.

"During the ceremony, I gave a soda to Jeffers that I'd laced with a sedative. He didn't have a chance. I was so angry at you. I was young and stupid and heartbroken."

I don't speak, my shock so complete I find it difficult to breathe. "You tried to kill me?"

She drops to her knees before me, taking my face in her hands. Tears sparkle in her cold eyes. "But you lived, Cleo. Don't you see? We're meant to be together."

Eyes wide, I don't respond. Taking it as an invitation, she leans forward and presses her lips to mine in a kiss. I freeze, a rabbit caught in the sights of a much smarter predator, and let her.

A phone rings upstairs, and she pulls back, breaking the kiss. Unfortunately, she doesn't leave. She takes my hand in hers and lays her head on my shoulder. I sit still, trying to comprehend the situation. What's next? Will she keep me in the basement until I die? And when, exactly, might that be? No, I can't die here. Maybe if I play along, I'll have a chance of making it out of here alive.

"I'm flattered, Macy. I did not know you felt that way and I only wish you would have said something sooner."

My voice shakes as I speak, but to my relief, she doesn't seem to notice. Instead, she beams at me.

"You don't know how relieved I am to hear you say that. I've been planning our life together for a long time. I bought this house for you—the flowers, did you see them? There's room for as many dahlias as you want. And I thought we could try for a baby. I found the perfect fertility clinic in Knoxville. Our life is going to be so perfect."

If she wants pursue parenthood with me and plant gardens, then maybe—just maybe—I can get out of this basement. I just need to play it right. I smile at her.

"The nursery is for us? I'd really like a baby, Macy."

"Then we'll have one." She leans forward to kiss me again, but I stop her with a hand on her chest.

"Can you take this off?" I gesture at the chain and smile at her.

"Once everything is finished, and I know you're going to stay." She smiles and stands, walking toward the stairs.

"I think I'll sleep down here with you tonight. We've got so much lost time to make up for. I want to soak up every second." She starts up the stairs, seemingly done with the conversation.

"Wait! Macy, wait!" She stops and walks back down a couple of stairs until she can see me again. I try to smile at her but fail.

"You're leaving?"

"There's a search party for you. I volunteered to help, and Ben's waiting for me at Dahlia's." My eyes must give me away because hers go hard. "Once he's taken care of, you'll be free to love just me."

I surge to my feet, running toward the stairs, grunting in pain as the chain stops my momentum.

"No, please don't hurt him, Macy. Please."

"He's done nothing but hurt you. You'll thank me later." Without another word, she walks up the stairs and shuts the door with a quiet click.

46

Like a wild animal caught in a snare, I test the limits of the chain, doing my best to drag the bed across the floor. It's made of iron and heavy, so I don't get far. Flat on my back, I press the heel of my foot against the frame and use all the strength I can muster in an attempt to separate the chain from the bed. After several minutes, I lay back, exhausted, tears pouring from my eyes and making a trail into my ears.

It's hopeless. I'm not strong enough to break the chain, and I don't have the key. I roll over to my side and stare at the stairs—so close, yet too far away. Macy has probably met up with Ben by now. My mind cycles through all the ways she might kill him, each one more painful than the last. *What if I never get to tell him how much I love him?*

By the time I see the paperclip on the floor, I'd lost Ben a dozen times over in my imagination. A hysterical laugh bounces around the room, shocking me when I realize it is mine. I crawl back to the bed and under it, reaching for the paperclip against the wall. It must have fallen from the photo of Vincent and me when she shoved it at me.

The tiny piece of metal is just out of reach, forcing me to stand and re-evaluate. I survey the room, looking for any object to use to pull it closer. I have to give it to her; she did a good job of escape-proofing the basement.

Determined, I crawl onto the bed and shove my arm into the gap between the bed and the wall. My fingers brush the tip, and I let out an excited, if not frustrated, laugh. Energized, I strain against the chain, pushing as far as I can to reach it. With a triumphant scream, my fingers close around it.

I sit up, my fingers trembling as I unfold the clip, making it as straight as I can. I purposely ignore the gash and blood oozing from my ankle. One problem at a time.

Thank God for insomnia is all I can say right now. Late-night scrolling on social media taught me four different ways to pick a pair of cuffs. Theoretically, anyway. I've never actually done it, but I've probably watched that video a half dozen times.

It takes a while, but eventually, I feel the cuff release from around my ankle. I don't waste time and hobble toward the stairs, grabbing a piece of the torn dress as I go. I test the knob, half afraid it's locked. A sigh of relief shudders out of me when it opens without issue. Macy must have thought I'd never make it far enough for it to be a problem. She underestimates me every time. Outside, the sky is darkening quickly. I'm running out of time.

Stumbling to the kitchen, I open cabinets in search of a first aid kit. I pause at the spice cabinet when I see a jar of paprika. A memory of Dahlia teaching me about plants in the kitchen washes over me.

"Cleo, remember this, okay? What is this spice?" Dahlia sits at the table, a small red jar in her hand.

"Umm. Cayenne?" I ask, complete attention on the woman in front of me.

"It's paprika. We use paprika a lot in the kitchen." My little head nods as she speaks. "But we can use paprika for other things too. Remember this, Cleo. If you're ever hurt, you can pack a wound with it. It's a temporary, yet effective, fix." She hands me the jar, my tiny hands closing around it in a fist.

Without hesitation, I grab the jar from the shelf and take a seat on Macy's pristine white couch. I pull my bleeding leg up on the cushion and watch as the blood seeps into it, turning white to crimson. My gaze follows the trail I left behind on the floor until it disappears around the corner to where I know it continues down the stairs into the basement.

Shit. That's a lot of blood. Okay, you can do this, Cleo. I use a nearby throw blanket to wipe away as much of it as possible and assess the wound. It's not too wide, but it is deep, the shape of it the perfect double crescent of a handcuff. I wipe my bloody hands on the wedding dress and flip off the lid of the paprika jar. I pour it over the wound, stopping to pack it in before pouring it again and again until I empty the jar. Tossing it aside, I wrap it up in the piece of dress I picked up as I left the basement.

With caution, I stand and test my weight on it. It

hurts, but it works. By the door, I see a pair of slippers and grab those as I run out the door, desperate to find Ben before it's too late.

47

Like the Bouchers, Macy lives just outside of town. Thankfully, her house is closer. I see the lights of the swinging bridge glittering through the trees before I reach it. Just as my feet hit the first plank, I see an all too familiar truck pull to a screeching stop on the other side. Ben.

He steps out, worry and relief in his eyes, and starts toward me, both of us at opposite ends of the bridge. I run, ignoring the pain and putting as much weight as I can on my uninjured leg.

"Cleo, just wait there. I'll come for you."

"Ben, listen, where's Macy?"

"Don't worry—she's okay. She's here; she's with me."

I see her then, her movements quick as she steps around the truck toward Ben, something silver shining in the light under the streetlamp.

"BEN!" I call out, but it's too late. I can only watch as

he falls to the ground, a carving knife lodged in his back. He doesn't move. The scream dies in my throat.

For a moment, I'm frozen, my eyes boring into him, willing him to stand, to save me. Macy darts toward the bridge, snapping me out of it. I'm on my own now. No one is coming to save me.

I turn as quickly as I can, limping back toward the safety of the other side. The bridge sways beneath us, our combined weight and pace making it dance. I don't make it far before she reaches me, tackling me to the wood. I kick out at her, desperate to remain apart.

Beneath us, the river rages, angry from the recent rains. Oblivious, Macy pulls me by my hair to stand. I'm bleeding again, but I do my best to keep my footing. This time, I keep eye contact, my eyes telling her how much I hate her.

"This is your last chance, Cleo. It's either me or death. Make your choice."

I gaze at the rushing water below us before letting my gaze follow the bridge to the bank where Ben's body lies still. I take a deep breath before looking back at Macy's triumphant face. Her body relaxes, her arms loosening around me.

I seize the opportunity, wrapping my arms around her, and dragging us over the rope railing and into the water below.

48

I lose sight of Macy in the water almost immediately. My last sighting is of her flailing arms in the water as she tries to swim toward shore. With water this high and fast, she'll tire quickly.

I do my best to remain calm, letting the current take me. I hold my breath when the water overtakes me and use minimal effort to find my way back to the surface. I think of Dahlia and feel her with me the whole way down.

"Relax. Don't tense up. Flip onto your back. That's good, Cleo. Stay calm. Breathe."

I let her voice guide me and do my best to take each breath with the flow of the river. For a while, all I do is breathe and pray.

Ahead, I see a change in the current and see my chance. I focus on Dahlia's voice, encouraging me, giving me strength.

"This is it, Cleo. When you hit the confluence, go for it. Swim as hard as you can toward the shore. Don't give up."

The conflux of the two rivers briefly interrupts the force of my movement downstream, giving me just enough time to kick toward shore. Again and again, I kick and stroke, fighting through the floodwater. Just before I reach the shore, I feel myself sinking and I gasp, swallowing water.

Fighting against the cramp in my right leg, I kick with all my might. Throwing an arm out, I make purchase against the grass, grabbing a root and holding it for dear life as the water pounds against me.

49

Macy's body was found three days after we went into the river. I'm not sorry to say I didn't attend her funeral. For my part, I spent a few days recovering in the hospital. After I was released, I stayed with Ben there and then moved into his apartment while he recovered.

We talked about everything—our hopes, our fears, our regrets. Ben admitted that he'd kept tabs on me, not because Dahlia had offered the information, but because he'd asked her about me often. He followed my art online, and while he had been angry at my betrayal with Vincent, he'd never stopped loving me.

When I lost my parents as a child, I never expected to find the love of a parent once again. Mariah and Vince came through for me in the days after Ben and I were attacked. More than that, when I moved in with Ben after he was released and continued to care for him, they embraced me.

Tate was, unsurprisingly, supportive of my decision

to remain in Shaconage and made my transition here simple and efficient. Reluctant to leave Ben during his recovery, I opted not to return to Arizona at all, at least for a while. My things should arrive at Dahlia's any day now.

It was easy to convince Netta to move into Dahlia's place with me. We need one another, and if this summer has taught me anything, time is too precious to waste. I had asked her once why Dahlia had erased all traces of me from the house. It turns out she had loaned my things to a gallery for an exhibit on local artists. Until the day she died, her love for me had never wavered.

Ben never did ask me to stay. It took me a while to realize it wasn't that he wouldn't. It was that he couldn't bring himself to ask me to make sacrifices for him. In the past, he'd left me, and while he had no intention of ever leaving me again, he needed it to be my choice. He needed me to ask him.

So, on a rainy Sunday afternoon in late September, I asked him to stay, and he did.

ACKNOWLEDGMENTS

When I first dreamed of Cleo and Vincent, I had no idea where this story would lead. There was no Ben or Macy or Dahlia. I simply had an idea that I was afraid to pursue. When I first started to turn this idea over in my head, I was working in social services and drowning in eighteen-hour workdays. Then, like everyone else, I had to adapt to the COVID-19 pandemic. When I wasn't investigating child abuse allegations, I was at home, alone, with only my dogs to keep me company. So I continued to dream of Cleo and eventually wrote the opening chapter.

Like many, the pandemic forced me to re-evaluate my life, to make myself a priority. I left my job and returned to school, becoming a nurse in 2021. In 2020, I met my husband, who encouraged me to write Cleo's story. There are so many people who have made this story possible and for that, I'll be forever grateful.

First, a huge thank you to the artists whose music inspired the playlist for this book. Particularly, I'd like to say thank you, Taylor Swift, for filling the last three years with endless inspiration. When I hit a rut in this story, your music never failed to pull me out of it. Your gifts have made mine better. Albums 6-10 have been my constant companions these last few years.

Thank you, Nana, for being my first reader. You never doubted I'd be able to finish Cleo's story and your feedback on my chapters made it an even better story. The boxes of romance novels and thrillers you'd send to my house monthly made me appreciate stories outside of the literary novels I was reading at school. If it weren't for those boxes of books, I would not be here today.

To my mom, who taught me to read. Though I don't remember the lessons, I'm grateful for them. Most three-year-old children aren't reading at that age, but you made sure I was- even if you regretted it when you wanted to have "spelling" conversations with Nanny Betty. As a result, I never missed out on any of the family drama/gossip.

To my friends: Sierra, Lindsay, Cortney, Mallory, and Jess. Thank you for being the first few to read this story, to love it as much as me. Your encouragement and excitement have been instrumental in building my confidence as a writer.

To Autumn, whose friendship made this book possible. Thank you for listening to Cleo's story repeatedly for the last three years. An even bigger thank you for saying, "Since it's COVID and you can't date in person anyway, I know this guy in PA who's perfect for you." Without your matchmaking skills, I would never have met my other half. I'm forever grateful you sent him my number. Life hasn't been the same since.

To Carmen, my editor. When you told me you loved Cleo and Ben, I think my heart exploded. Those simple words made all the hard work and tears worth it. Your support, edits, and cheerleading have been invaluable to me these last few months.

To Margaret, my copyeditor. Thank you for catching all the little mistakes and turning this story into something polished.

To Samantha, my first author friend. I'm so glad I came across your TikTok and requested to beta-read The Aspect of Essence. It's nice to know that when I'm up late at night writing, you probably are too. Thank you for being one of the first readers of Cleo's story and for loving her as much as I do.

Finally, to Shane, my wonderful husband. How to put into words how you've changed my life? To even attempt to do it justice would be impossible. I'll say only this: From that first text message, I've never been the same. Thank you for your unwavering belief that I could write something that others would love; for the conviction, from day one, that I would someday be a published author.

RESOURCES

If you've experienced domestic violence, sexual assault, or any other type of violence, you are a survivor and I'm so proud of you. Below are resources available to you at no cost. These services are 24/7.

The National Domestic Violence Hotline: 800-799-7233 or Text START to 88788
https://www.thehotline.org/?utm_source=google&utm_medium=organic&utm_campaign=domestic_violence

Love is Respect—National Teen Dating Abuse Hotline
Hotline: 1 (866) 331—9474 or Text: 22522

Website: https://www.loveisrespect.org/

StrongHearts Native Helpline
Hotline: 1 (844) 762—8483

This service is available Monday--Friday, 9:00 am to 5:30 pm CST via phone.

Website: https://strongheartshelpline.org

National Sexual Assault Hotline: 1-800-656-4673
Rape, Abuse, and Incest National Network (RAINN) – National Sexual Assault Hotline
Hotline: 1 (800) 656--4673
Online Chat Available: https://www.rainn.org/

National Human Trafficking Hotline: 1-888-373-7888; Text: 233733

Website: https://humantraffickinghotline.org/en

ChildHelp National Child Abuse Hotline: 1 (800) 422—4453

Website: https://www.childhelp.org/

Gay, Lesbian, Bisexual, and Transgender National Hotline
Hotline: 1 (888) 843—4564

Website: https://www.lgbthotline.org/

These resources, and others, can also be found at https://victimconnect.org/resources/national-hotlines/.

ABOUT THE AUTHOR

Roxie lives in Pennsylvania with her husband and two dogs. Most nights, she can be found on TikTok with her writing group, Distracted Inklings. When she's not writing, Roxie likes to go on long walks, ride as many rollercoasters as she can in one day, and obsess over the depravity of orcas. Roxie is the author of Through a Mirror Darkly, which is set in The Great Smoky Mountains where she grew up. Upcoming releases include This Tangled Web, the first novel in the Jude Amarante Casefiles, Gemma Stone & The Missing Dragon Egg, the first novella in the Magic Defense Series, as well as Kiss Me in the Dark, a standalone romantic suspense.

This Tangled Web: A Jude Amarante Casefile

Gemma Stone and the Missing Dragon Egg: A Magic Defense
Series novella (Releases 2.19.2024)

Kiss Me in the Dark (Releases 3.25.2024)